Aram's Notebook

Aram's Notebook

A NOVEL

Maria Àngels Anglada

TRANSLATED AND WITH AN INTRODUCTION
BY ARA H. MERJIAN

SWAN ISLE PRESS
CHICAGO

Maria Àngels Anglada (1930–99) was an award-winning twentieth-century Catalan novelist and poet. Her books include *Les closes* and *El violí d'Auschwitz*.

Ara H. Merjian is an art historian and professor of Italian Studies at New York University. He is the author and editor of numerous books.

Swan Isle Press, Chicago 60611
© 2024 by Swan Isle Press
© 2024 by the Literary Estate of Maria Àngels Anglada
Translation & Introduction © 2024 by Ara H. Merjian

All rights reserved. Published 2024.
Printed in the United States of America
First Edition

28 27 26 25 24   1 2 3 4 5

ISBN-13: 978-1-9610560-3-9

Quadern d'Aram was originally published by Educaula 62 / Grup62 (2009).

Cover image: The Greek coral diver Ioannis Mastoros (uno de los empleados de la empresa de buzos Jorge Kontos) on the Catalan coast, with the town of Cadaqués in the background, winter 1932. Photo courtesy of Pere Vehí Contos, Cadaqués. All rights reserved.

Library of Congress Cataloging-in-Publication Data
Names: Anglada, Maria Àngels, 1930–1999, author. | Merjian,
    Ara H., 1974– translator.
Title: Aram's Notebook : a novel / Maria Àngels Anglada ; translated
    by Ara H. Merjian.
Other titles: Quadern d'Aram. English
Description: Chicago : Swan Isle Press, 2024. | Includes bibliographical
    references.
Identifiers: LCCN 2024019334 | ISBN 9781961056039 (trade paperback)
Subjects: LCSH: Armenian Genocide, 1915–1923—Fiction. | BISAC:
    FICTION / Historical / 20th Century / General | FICTION / World
    Literature / Turkey | LCGFT: Historical fiction. | Novels.
Classification: LCC PC3942.1.N45 Q3313 2024 | DDC 849/.9354—dc23/
    eng/20240614
LC record available at https://lccn.loc.gov/2024019334

Swan Isle Press gratefully acknowledges that this edition was made possible, in part, with grants and generous support from the following:

THE COMMUNITY OF LITERARY MAGAZINES AND PRESSES |
    CAPACITY-BUILDING GRANT
ILLINOIS ARTS COUNCIL AGENCY
EUROPE BAY GIVING TRUST
OTHER KIND DONORS

The paper used in this publication meets the minimum requirements of the American National Standard of Information Sciences—Permanence of Paper for Printed Library Materials.

Contents

Translator's Introduction

As the first major Catalan literary work translated into the Armenian language, Maria Àngels Anglada's novel *El quadern d'Aram* was greeted with great fanfare at the start of the new millennium in Armenia. In both her literary and journalistic corpus, Àngels Anglada had already proven to be what might be called a "committed" author. Her writing takes up a number of different but interrelated threads: human and civil rights, the protection of minoritarian cultures and languages, the rights of women, and the preservation of memory in the wake of genocide and diaspora. In addition to the salient characteristics of her prose and poetry, this sense of moral rectitude made Àngels Anglada one of the most prominent figures of late twentieth-century Catalan letters. Theatrical performances, special journal issues, and entire books have since been dedicated to her place in the Catalan literary tradition.

With *Aram's Notebook*, she entered a different pantheon: that of foreign authors moved to address Armenia's early twentieth-century tragedy through fiction. That pantheon has long been limited; for decades, it contained a single individual: the Austrian-Bohemian novelist of Jewish descent Franz Werfel. His landmark novel *The Forty Days of Musa Dagh* (1933) centers on Armenian resistance to deportation and massacre in a mountain community of southern Anatolia—an emblematic fragment of a much larger catastrophe. At nearly a thousand pages, Werfel's tome quickly exceeded in significance its length and heft. As intuited by none other than Hitler himself, the Armenian Genocide famously prefigured elements of the Nazi Final Solution, as well as the wider world's initial refusals of acknowledgment. It is certainly not coincidental that *The Forty Days of Musa Dagh* was a popular read among internees of the Warsaw Ghetto, who found it an inspiration for their own acts of resistance.

It fell to another German-speaking author of Jewish origin to pen the century's next literary treatment of the genocide, published more than fifty years later. Winner of the prestigious Alfred Döblin Prize, Edgar Hilsenrath's *The Story of the Last Thought* (1989) likewise takes as the focus of its story a single Anatolian village. Though often compared to Werfel's novel, Hilsenrath's book incorporates the (further) internal narrative device of the fairy tale, along with other literary genres, which serves to mediate the protagonists' relationship to memory and its transmission. These genres call attention to the role of oral history in the genocide's afterlife.

Aram's Notebook brings literature to the fore by way of plot and character alike. The novel unfolds in the form of a diary kept by its eponymous fictional author. His father, Vahe—who is missing, and presumably dead or imprisoned—is modeled on the Armenian poet Daniel Varoujan (1884–1915), one of the genocide's most prominent literary victims. Àngels Anglada punctuates her narrative with a range of citations from Armenia's rich literary past, from the medieval poet Nahapet Kuchak to modernist poets like Hrand Nazariantz and Varoujan himself. Born in the village of Perknig near modern-day Sivas (in what is now Turkey), Varoujan was educated by the Mekhitarist Catholic order on the island of San Lazzaro, Venice, and subsequently at the University of Ghent in Belgium. His return to the Armenian community and his service as the principal of the St. Gregory the Illuminator School in Constantinople was cut short by his detention in 1915 and murder later that same year. Varoujan's stirring, controversial *Pagan Songs* (1912) remains a touchstone of Armenia's secular modernism and inflects Àngels Anglada's narrative at various points.

As a historical novel, the volume draws on scholarship of the genocide and incorporates passages from contemporary texts (see the author's note). In addition to an intense personal interest in Varoujan's poetry— brought to fruition in a posthumously published volume of translations—Àngels Anglada also assimilated some autobiographical elements into the story's framing. She first became interested in Armenian culture and literature after the *Revista del Centre de Lectura*, a journal based in the city of Reus, published Catalan translations of poetry by Hrand Nazariantz in 1921. She then nourished this interest with French translations of modern Armenian authors by the French-Swiss scholar Vahé Godel (whose first name she also borrowed for the novel's fictionalized Varoujan).

Catalonia's connections with Armenia date back to the fourteenth-century travels of the theologian and philosopher Ramon Llull to the Kingdom of Cilicia, then flourishing on the Mediterranean coast. As the first work of Catalan literature to be translated into Armenian, *Aram's Notebook* revisits that distant connection by referring to the presence and absence of the sea in twentieth-century Armenian life: the geographic connection to the Black Sea lost with the Treaty of Sèvres in 1920, and an equally bitter series of Mediterranean exiles in the wake of genocide.

It is the Mediterranean that ties together so many of Àngels Anglada's interests, anchored by her training in classical philology and extending into twentieth-century history. Aram goes to work for the Kontos family, a clan of Greek coral fishermen plying their trade along the Mediterranean coast. They are based on an actual Greek family bearing the name of Kontos, who settled in the port town of Cadaqués in the 1920s from the island of Symi (the same as in the novel). The narrative begins, in fact, with the recent sighting on Catalan shores of a lizard native to the Dodecanese islands—an inexplicable migration of species that speaks to other historical "resettlements." It also alludes to Àngels Anglada's own discovery of Armenian poetry via translation upon her arrival to the city of Reus—a different sort of displacement.

This and other elements of the novel continually test the boundaries between fact and fiction. Since the Armenian Genocide's history has for so long been haunted by the specter of denial—most notoriously by the modern successors of the Ottoman state—its fictional literary evocations have proven especially fraught. The publication of Micheline Aharonian Marcom's novel *Three Apples Fell from Heaven* in 2001 sparked polemics—mostly from within the Armenian community—as to whether fiction could or should be used to deal with the genocide. By "fictionalizing" its events—even within the frame of a historical narrative—Marcom was thought by some to undermine its factual status. The author herself defended her approach in an interview published in the Autumn 2002 issue of *Ararat* as wanting to

> bring to life a boy whose life and history, if you will, [went] unrecorded, as did so much of the Armenian experience during and after the Genocide. I also became interested in this: how History affects the "common man" and how this man is left out of the history books. Of course, for Armenians living in the diaspora we know that our history has been denied and often erased by [other versions of] history, so we understand this viscerally[.] . . . [W]riters and artists have the obligation more than ever to seek and tell the truth, to uncover the lies of power, to tell the stories of the powerless, the unvoiced, unknown narratives.

Àngels Anglada undertakes precisely such a narrative, voiced by a boy who might just as well have existed—*did* in fact exist, in various iterations and incarnations, however anonymous or unvoiced. Indeed, after the publication of Àngels Anglada's (similarly fictional) *The Violin of Auschwitz* in 1994, an individual contacted the author to share a personal, familial account that was uncannily consonant with the novel's details. As in *The Violin of Auschwitz*, *Aram's Notebook* merges historical documents—news dispatches, articles—with speculations about their bearing on individuals and community alike. A similar impetus drives the pursuit (and theorization) of speculative fiction by the cultural historian Saidiya Hartman, whose research restores the literary and personal expression denied to young African American girls in their lifetimes. Hartman has been nourished by the microhistorical work of scholars like Carlo Ginzburg and Clifford Geertz. Focusing on the fictional family of a real intellectual further grounds the cultural and literary fluency of the novel's characters in actual example. Like Maryk, the fictional Aram's mother, Varoujan's widow did, in fact, go on to edit and disseminate the murdered poet's unpublished work.

Àngels Anglada's novel can be characterized as a book for young adults (indeed, it first appeared in the "young readers" series of its original Catalonian publisher). Yet it speaks to a far broader audience. Not unlike the real and more famous diary of Anne Frank, its journal entries issue from an adolescent in the throes of persecution. While Aram's mother, Maryk, takes up his journal at various points in the narrative, it is the young, imagined Aram who gives the story its impetus and principal voice—a voice rushing to record the horrors unfolding around a fragmenting family; a voice intent upon snatching adolescent pleasures from the teeth of history's jaws; the voice of a son left fatherless just as he comes into manhood himself. Incidentally, Aram's close rapport with Iorgos, the son of the Kontos clan, recalls in many ways the Greek and Armenian friendship at the heart of Elia Kazan's film *America, America* (1963). It also speaks to the contemporary and interrelated exile of Greek (especially Pontic) populations, likewise former subjects in Ottoman lands. Once again, the emigration of the real-life Kontos clan from Symi to Cadaqués in 1917—in the midst of world war and the death throes of Ottoman aggression—anchors the novel's traversals in historical reality.

As a window on early twentieth-century Armenian life, *Aram's Notebook* manages to be instructive without being pedantic. Readers young and old will find in it an introduction to some of western Armenian culture's most recognizable traditions and textures: cuisine, holy sites, folk customs, terms of address and endearment. Indeed, Àngels Anglada seems intent not only on recounting a series of events but on conveying the rituals attendant upon them, however casual or quotidian. Thus, we read not only about the acquittal of the Armenian patriot Soghomon Tehlirian—and his symbolic act of revindication against the genocide's architects—but also the community *khorovadz* that might have greeted it: the grilling of meat (especially lamb) for collective celebration. The haste and urgency of Aram and Maryk's escape is likewise underscored by the preparation of *lavash*—a flat, unleavened bread easily stored and transported (which also recalls, particularly in the context of exile, the baking of unleavened flatbread by the Israelites of the Old Testament). We learn, too, of Vahe's studies on the island of San Lazzaro in the Venetian lagoon—a long-standing outpost of Armenian religious education in Western Europe—as well as the lesser-known resettlement of refugees in Italy's Pugliese peninsula.

For most of the last century, the legacy of the Armenian Genocide has been held hostage to the vagaries of geopolitics. Archival, juridical, and forensic evidence proved no match for the contingencies of trade deals and the policies of denial, prevarications, and partial admissions; the consensus of an overwhelming majority of international historians took a back seat to the dictates of state interests. In more recent years, the tide has shifted to some degree. In April 2021, Joe Biden became the first sitting president of the United States to recognize the genocide officially as such, concluding—if not resolving —decades of rhetorical contortions. When the state of Mississippi became the fiftieth state to acknowledge the genocide, it also declared April "Genocide Awareness and Prevention Month." Though hardly consequential in geopolitical terms, this English translation of Àngels Anglada's novel offers some fresh consolation of its own, steeped in the salt of the Mediterranean and of the tears shed across its twentieth-century surface, in suffering and solace alike.

This translation's long gestation has benefited from the encouragement, friendship, and good cheer of several individuals: Nuria Berlinguer, Bob Davidson, Sergi Rivero Navarro, Joan Ramon Resina, Maria Roura, Santiago Zabala, and especially Veronica Raya Díaz and Jordi Falgàs. My sincere thanks to Maria Ohannesian Saboundjian and to the heirs of Maria Àngels Anglada for their help in bringing out this volume. Pat Lunn's meticulous revisions of the translation have made it stronger, as has David Rade's editorial savvy and careful stewardship. I am indebted to Elizabeth Ellingboe for her astute queries and copy edits. Pere Vehi Contos kindly granted permission to reproduce the stunning photograph of the diver Ioannis Mastoros in the Bay of Cadaqués. I dedicate this translation to the memory of my mother, Haiganoush Agnes Merjian (1937–2023), daughter of genocide survivors, whose love and laughter honored what cannot be forgotten.

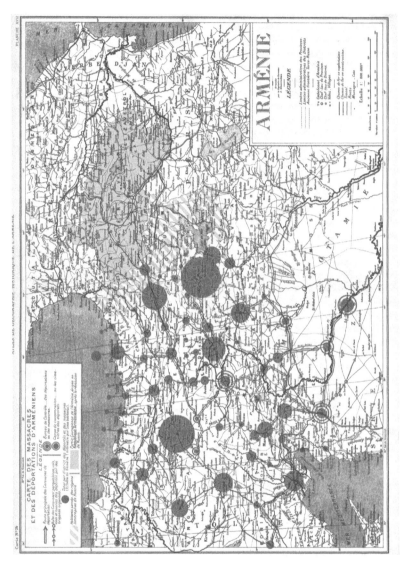

FIGURE I

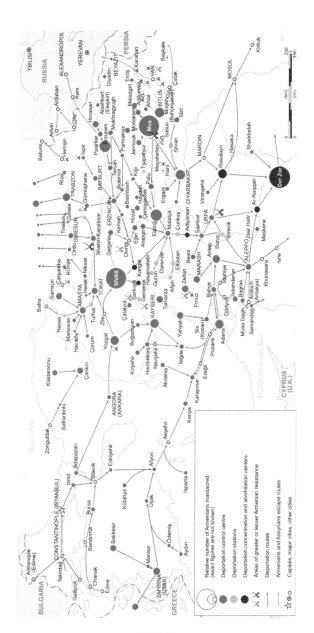

FIGURE 2

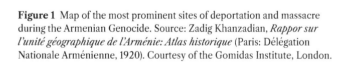

Figure 1 Map of the most prominent sites of deportation and massacre during the Armenian Genocide. Source: Zadig Khanzadian, *Rappor sur l'unité géographique de l'Arménie: Atlas historique* (Paris: Délégation Nationale Arménienne, 1920). Courtesy of the Gomidas Institute, London.

Figure 2 Map of the Armenian Genocide. Vahagn Avedian after J. Naslian and B. H. Harutyunyan, in Robert H. Hewswen, *Armenia: A Historical Atlas* (University of Chicago Press, 2011).

Aram's Notebook

I

Agama stellio

My grandson Adrià is crazy about animals. He seems to know every species and its behavior, and he observes them patiently. He's quite skilled at catching them alive, too. He always sets them free afterwards, safe and sound—except, that is, for the unlucky octopi he's supplied for our dinners all summer. So, while we were living on Rhodes, it came as no surprise when he managed to catch—just for a few moments—one of the strange lizards native to the island. They measure about two hands long and stand erect on their legs, much taller than ordinary lizards. Their striking color is somewhere between brown and gold, and they sometimes go by the name "Rhodes dragon," since they differ slightly from the Cycladic lizards. But their scientific name, from what I gather, is *Agama stellio*.

I decided to write this tale in Rhodes, from which you can make out the island of Symi and, even closer, the Turkish coast. And so I begin it with the name of the hardy and slippery "dragon" from this sunny isle. And perhaps also because stories sometimes prove harder to grasp than the *Agama stellio*. And, like that agile reptile, they often show themselves and, once you've caught

3

sight of them, disappear. I realize now that years before I ever went to Rhodes and Symi, I had already made out the story of Aram, Iorgos, and Maryk—nameless, hazy. When did I first learn about the poetry of Hrand Nazariantz? Was it in the Catalan village of Roses, where Constantinos Kontos Jr. showed me a notebook belonging to his grandfather, a Greek coral fisherman from Cadaqués?

More than a notebook, it was actually a small book, given to Constantinos's grandfather by the mutual aid society of the Greek Orthodox Church of Marseille. Such organizations were quite necessary back in the days when there was still no national social assistance. Along with that volume, I got hold of a thick manuscript written in characters I couldn't make out—not even a stroke. But I made a photocopy and held on to it, with the intention of finding someone who could help me decipher it.

The notebook languished for years among all kinds of things in one of my desk drawers, until recently. On our way back from Rhodes, we'd planned to stay a day and a night in Athens. I got up at the crack of dawn, as I always do when I'm in Greece, and as soon as the bookstores opened—some as early as 8:00 a.m.—I bought myself a couple of volumes of Armenian poetry translated into French at Kaufmann's bookstore. I was in luck: the beautiful calligraphy of the original Armenian poems was very similar to the writing in my hidden notebook. At the very least, I now knew where the writers had come from. And their diary—for the notebook could be nothing less—would help me to write a book about the Armenians, as I'd just decided to do on Rhodes.

A further surprise lay in store: my friend Daco, a naturalist from the Empordà region in Catalonia and a specialist in lizards, published an article claiming, in detail, that he had observed a previously unsighted *Agama stellio* on a stone wall in Cadaqués. He couldn't explain it, he simply reported on it. How had a lizard from Rhodes found itself at the other end of the Mediterranean? A mystery of nature, which even specialists could not account for . . .

Good fortune continued to nurture my persistence. Through my friend Ramon, I came to meet Maria Ohannesian, who deciphered the writing in Aram's book. Maria is an Armenian from Argentina, settled in Catalonia, who is a servant to the memory of her grandparents and their ancient tongue. Without Maria, I would not have been able to introduce you to Aram, Maryk, and Iorgos. Aram's notebook contains hardly any dates, perhaps because nightmares seem to occur outside of time, and his exile was a nightmare, though a real and terrible one. Further on, there are a few dates. In any case, the events that it records occurred between the years 1914 and 1925. I should also tell you that for Aram's father, my Vahe, I have taken inspiration from the great Armenian poet, Daniel Varoujan (1884–1915).

II
Aram and Iorgos

It's hard for us nowadays to imagine what Aram and Iorgos looked like when they dove into the deep blue of
the Gulf of Sirte, off the coast of Tunisia. The lovely
descriptions of modern divers—who with their swim
fins, like duck feet, and portable air tanks look like
bird-fish—don't help us at all. The situation in the 1920s
was quite different.

"I floated weightlessly," writes the poet and scuba diver
Antonio Ribera, "gliding over a dreamscape of jag-
ged rocks covered with algae, mysterious reefs half-
hidden by jellyfish, as we passed through clouds of fish."

Instead, the two young friends and work partners—
one Greek and one Armenian—look like little sea monsters: they've put on the heavy bronze helmets, which
they can see out of because in the front there's a kind
of glass window. And a rubber tube, like an exceedingly
long umbilical cord, connects them to the oxygen tank
above, located for this particular expedition on the boat
Dimitrios. Rather than floating, they move heavily, as if
they were lumbering over the rocks. But they always obey
Kostas's golden rule: "Never dive alone!"

Silence surrounds them. Colored fish move about, weightless in their element, while above the surface of the sea shimmers like a mirror. But the divers have no time to admire the undulating movements of the silver sea bream nor even, today, the red of the coral. They have other things to focus on. Up on deck, the guide pays close attention to the movements of their air hose: two quick tugs mean "more air," while four tugs mean "bring us up!" But they won't need to call for tools, because in the pouch on the front of their rubber suits each has a hammer.

They've now reached twenty meters; they won't go any deeper. They know this will be their last dive in this zone. If they can't find the remains of the boat they've been after for days, then tomorrow they'll try in another spot. This is what the boss has decided. That's why, once they've passed through the moving mirror of the surface, they don't really see the rocks that look to be covered with little yellow flowers, anthozoa, while the dark seaweed sways unceasingly, like hair tousled by the north wind. They have only half an hour, and they don't want to waste energy. They're young, but they've witnessed more than one accident.

They move slowly, walking along the rocky bottom "like animals rampant." Their leaden suits weigh about seventy kilos. Aram follows his more knowledgeable companion and soon realizes that Iorgos has found something important. He easily translates the sign Iorgos has made with his fingers after putting something in his bag. "Come here, and then up," he motions.

But what is it that Aram and Iorgos are looking for

on behalf of their boss? We have to go a few years back in time to find this out, to 1907, to be exact. The year a Greek sponge fisherman, like Iorgos himself, discovered, he said, a sunken ship full of . . . cannons. But it wasn't cannons that he saw blurred by the currents; it was re-splendent Greek columns of Pentelic marble—slender and beautiful, as he was able to see after exhausting dives and a serious campaign of exploration. And sculptures, goblets, and trivets, too . . . The Great War had inter-rupted exploration, and the exact location of the sunken ship, too, was lost. But maybe Iorgos had found it again!

Aram goes to his side, and his eyes widen: he sees Iorgos fitting a tiny sculpture into his bag, its exact con-tours hard to make out. He would love to take something up as well, but time is up; he loosens a fragment of mar-ble from the wood, and together they signal ascent. Now they move slowly towards the surface, today a swaying, wavering, web of light. Now, exhausted, they clamber back on board the *Dimitrios*, and then, free from the heavy helmet, the pick, and the rubber suit, the Greek diver reveals the sea's treasure to his companions. The expedition's archaeologist almost starts dancing with joy upon seeing, through the cataracts of so many years, the profile of the sculpted face, the plaited hair. Iorgos has found, without a doubt, the sunken Greek ship loaded with treasures from Attica. He has before him the profile of the goddess of love, the face of Aphrodite.

"What you've brought up, Aram," the archaeologist remarks smilingly, "is the top of a column."

The two friends smile, tired and satisfied. There will be work for days now, thinks Aram, saying nothing. Iorgos, in contrast, chatters and waves his arms, as if showing with his hands the discoveries that await below. Now, out of their helmets and underwater gear, the two boys look very unlike one another: the Armenian is shorter than his friend, with eyes that are jet black, perhaps a bit sad. Iorgos is one of those blond Greeks sometimes to be found on the islands, and his laughing eyes are blue-green like the waters around Symi.

The delicious aroma of lobster wafts over them: their companions found lobsters in a cove. The ship's cook has grilled them in the galley, and there's enough for everybody. They wash down the meal with good wine, and the calm sea adds to the celebration of today's find.

III
Aram's Diary: Athens

The Shepherds of Van
  —Hear, sister roses: our branches are not there,
  disaster's scythe has cut them down.
  They were thirsty, the herds, and they drank
  from springs and rivers that dripped blood.
  Parched, they died by the fountains.

HRAND NAZARIANTZ

Sometimes I wake up in the night and cry out. Or maybe I have a nightmare, and I cry out in my sleep. I'm fifteen years old, but I can't help it. I cry out for my father, cry out his name: Vahe, Vahe! I cry out for my grandmother, my two sisters: Sofia, Yaneh!

Then my mother, Maryk, hears me and comes to my side. She takes me in her arms like when I was little, she runs her fingers over my sweaty forehead, her hand as cool as the roses from her garden in Trebizond.

"Shhh, Aram, my son. It's late, son, go to sleep. Don't wake the others."

Listening to her, I'm reminded of the lullaby she sang to me as a child—I didn't learn it then, of course, but when she was rocking my baby sisters. It's the same one, she told me, that her mother sang to her:

> Sleep, my child, and close your eyes.
> Let your pretty eyes grow drowsy.
> Sleep and make me sleepy, too,
> Mother of God, bring him slumber.
> Lu-lu, my son, lu-lu, lullaby.
> Now the baby is falling asleep.

But now I wouldn't want her to sing it. I'm grown up, and, besides, the other people might wake up. Because we're not sleeping alone; we're a bunch of women, children, a few old folks—many died along the way—the men who haven't yet emigrated. We ended up sleeping in the opera house in Athens; others are in hotels on the coast, on the islands, in covered markets, in convents . . . I don't know how many of us are left. Nobody really knows, I don't think.

I always remember my father, more than the other people in my family, though I love them all. I think about my father, who's dead, who must have died with his weapons in his hands, I'm sure, fighting our Turkish assassins. In spite of things I've heard, I can't imagine that he died any other way, brave as he was, though he might've looked skinny and weak, with his eyeglasses. I don't want to think about my sisters or my grandmother. We know for sure how they were killed, but I don't want to think about it, or write it down.

My father is a poet. I don't say "was," because poets last forever. He'd already published two books, and I'm afraid that all the copies have been lost or burned, except for the ones that Mother took with her when we left, she and I, for Van. She's never let those books out of her sight on all the trips and treks we've had to make. She took them for the pleasure of having them, not because she expected anything bad to happen, she told me.

I remember all the preparations for our trip and how nice and sunny it was the morning we left home the last happy morning, the last day I saw my sisters, my grandmother, and my father, Vahe. My parents' last embrace, my sisters' and my grandmother's kisses.

"Maryk, everything is fine," said my grandmother. "Don't worry about the girls or Vahe."

"Or your roses," added my father. "You'll find them well cared for when you come back."

Because we lived in a house with a garden—small but full of rose bushes. My mother used to say that they were Anatolian roses, the sweetest-smelling roses in the world. And now we're moving farther and farther away from everything, because of a vow that my mother made. I'd been very sick the year before with pneumonia—at death's door—and my mother, who's very religious, had promised that if I recovered, then the two of us would make a pilgrimage to the monastery of Narek, near Lake Van, and to the Cathedral of the Holy Cross on the island of Aghtamar. A long and complicated trip, up to the foot of the mountains. That's why we joined a group of people who were going there that year. It was the centennial (I don't remember which one) of Saint Gregory the Illuminator.

I would miss many weeks of school, but I was still young, and my father—who was a professor of Greek and French—had given his approval.

"When you get back," he said, "I'll give you intensive classes every day and get you caught up."

He made me take a couple of books, to study whenever I had the time. My mother had relatives in the province of Van, some cousins who would give us a place to stay. If it hadn't been for that I don't think Father would have let us travel so far. Saddest of all was my grandmother, as if she'd had a premonition. It was hard for her to let go of me.

"Goodbye, Aram! God bless you!"

I never heard her voice again. Once in a while I dream of her. It's still too painful for me to write memories of our family. Maybe in the future I will. But now I want to record an important fact: I've found a friend. I didn't have any here; almost all the boys are much younger than me.

I missed the sea so much that I decided to go to the port—on foot, because we don't have money to do it any other way. I walked a long way, asking directions, until I reached the sea at the port of Piraeus. I'd never seen such a busy place. Trebizond was very different, never mind Lake Van. I love to swim, and my father got me started when I was little, just six—and not just in the sea, but also in the Deguimen River, which is harder. A few times we'd gone as far as the Zigana Pass, in the mountains, and my father would say, "You swim like a salmon." He said it was not because I was swimming upstream (like salmon do, he explained), but because I loved to swim in rough water. When I was nine I would swim behind waterfalls and underwater and everything, until my eyes would sting.

So now I've found a friend like me. His name is Iorgos, and he's Greek, from the island of Symi. He knows how to dive, and he's a sponge fisherman. He started talking with me, and we became friends right away. He bought me an orangeade and told me all about his home and his island and his uncle Kostas. He also gave me half his lunch, which I thought was delicious, especially the bread and the grilled meat. I didn't realize how long I'd been there, listening to him and talking.

"Wow, it's so late! I've gotta go, my mother will worry."

Iorgos went part of the way with me, and we agreed to meet again, tomorrow. I don't mind walking to the port.

Today they handed out clothes, which we sure needed. My mother couldn't patch mine anymore, especially at the elbows and knees. She says they're from an American organization called Near Eastern Relief, the one that runs the orphanages for thousands of Armenian children. I got a brand-new sweater and a pair of pants that are too long for me, but Maryk will hem them to my size. Also some shoes and socks. Maryk will have to fix the dress they gave her, too, because she's so thin now.

I put on my sweater right away to go back to the port. Not the shoes; my mother says they have to last a long time. Iorgos and I had agreed on the exact spot where we'd meet, and he took me to meet his uncle and the other sailors. They're all from Symi, except for one, who's from here. And I ate dinner with them on their ship, a really good dinner. It'd been a long time since I'd had such good lamb. They also gave me a huge dish of stewed octopus with rice.

"Eat, boy. You must've been hungry for a while," Iorgos's uncle said.

"Yeah, but I'm full, thanks."

"You're grown up, have some wine. It's from Rhodes," he added.

After dinner they showed me the whole boat, which isn't new or very big, but a good sailor and well made, "built entirely at the Symi shipyards," as Iorgos told me proudly.

"Do you see that icon? It's Saint Nicholas, protector of all sailors. Whenever we run into danger, he pulls us through—or Saint Michael Panormitis, the patron saint of the island."

Between dinner and talking with the sailors from Symi, time flew by. What a difference from the long, endless afternoons in the refugee camp when the weather was bad, or the even longer winters in Yerevan!

I hadn't felt so good since we fled Van, so long ago. They couldn't stand the Turks either. They asked me about all kinds of things, and they told me about their projects. But the best thing is that these projects . . . include me! They've gotten out of the sponge business, which wasn't going too well, and they're going to fish for coral—red coral. Iorgos will teach me to dive, and later they'll give me work on board. They made me a promise, and I'm sure they'll keep it.

Iorgos has told them how well I can swim and how much I love the sea. He told them that I know how to swim underwater, holding my breath, and I think he probably overdid it. But I am attracted to the sea, even now that I know how my grandmother and the girls died. The sea isn't to blame, men are, the blasted Turks. The sea is innocent. So I'll work with the Greek coral fishermen, I'll do whatever needs doing. They're going to Marseille to sell the coral, they told me, the city where we're going to live! My mother is waiting for a letter about work to go there. A friend from Van, a relative of her cousin who already works there, will send for her and is already looking for a place for us to live with the help of the ANCHA (the American National Committee to Aid Homeless Armenians). There's a lot of Armenian families, he says, in that French city, and they've started an Association of Compatriots of Van to help one other. Maryk will be able to sew at home for the same company where our friend works. It won't be long, she says, before we leave, with a whole group of other Armenians. She says that, strange as it seems, it'll be easier to get news there about some of our friends and relatives who might've survived the massacres, maybe even Father. I miss him so much. All we know is that he's on the list of the dead, no more, but who knows? What if by chance or by the will of God he survived with other rebels in Musa Dagh? No, if he were alive, he would have found us by now, we would've heard something, and he wouldn't be on the list of dead. Father died a hero, fighting for the Armenia he loved so much.

Soon we'll leave again for a new city. Our friend from Van, who was able to find his family again, has sent us a letter with the address and everything in Marseille. We'll be living on the rue Longue-des-Capucins, which isn't far from the port. That makes me happy. He says we'll have two small bedrooms, a kitchen, and a balcony. So my mother will be able to grow roses in pots on the balcony. She also has a sewing job lined up: the uniform company will pay for her sewing machine and deduct it from her salary little by little. Maryk is very brave and even smiled a little when she said, "We'll be fine, Aram, you'll see. We'll find friends from Van, and maybe even friends from Trebizond. There's a Greek church there, too, and you can sing in the choir." Because my voice has already changed, and everybody says I have a good bass voice.

It might seem strange, but we refugees often sing here in Athens. We don't sing to forget our sorrows; we do it to remember our songs. There's a music teacher, kind of old, who gets us together two evenings a week, those of us who love music, and has us sing. He teaches us church music, wedding marches, popular songs. I've loved music ever since I was little.

"Our son will be a musician," Father would say, before the war. "Look what a good ear he has, how he learns songs after hearing them only once."

I remember it was during the good times; he said it one evening when we were eating in the little garden because the weather was so nice. Father was sitting in a wicker chair after supper, and while my mother and grandmother cleared the table, he read us some new poems. He had a beautiful, deep voice, though it wasn't very strong. The last rays of sunlight lit up the glasses they hadn't yet collected, and the hidden crickets accompanied my father's verses, knowing that dusk was approaching. The one I liked best was "Benediction," which I know by heart.

> Let me pour wheat into your hands,
> my valiant son, my centurion.
> . . .
> Let me pour wheat over your head,
> my beloved grandson, my springtime staff.

But my father won't see him, his grandson, even if I ever have a son.

> Let me pour wheat into your hands,
> My girl, my rose, wreath of my tomb.

How many times have I seen my mother, whenever she's not sewing on our old clothes, reading and reciting Father's poems. She keeps some of his writings nearby, which she knows by heart. If everything goes well, and I find a lot of coral and earn a lot of money, I'll rent an apartment or a house with a garden for my mother, where she can raise her roses and sit in the evening and read Vahe's verses. Because I'm going to be a coral fisherman, a diver, not a musician. My mother was afraid when I told her, but my friend and his uncle will know how to calm her down. They'll explain the precautions we take and how the boss will keep an eye on us so nothing bad happens. We've escaped from worse things, Maryk and I, before now.

An example: my mother's cousin, the one from Van, died in the mountains while we were fleeing towards Russia, like so many others. Her heart gave out and stopped all of a sudden. But her husband, son, and little daughter were able to make it to Etchmiadzin, worn out and dead tired, like us. But we were safe. So if we escaped the dangers of that horrible escape, why shouldn't I be lucky with the sea, my old friend? I just have to convince my mother, who always wants me by her side.

Today Iorgos told me a lot about his family and their island, Symi. He says he misses it when he's far away, and now it'll be a while before he can go there, but he hopes to return for his big sister's wedding. He showed me a photo of them all: his father, his mother, all dressed in black, his sister Electra with her fiancé Mikael, and his little sister. They're standing in front of a big, beautiful monastery, Panormitis, by the edge of the sea. The monastery, he says, is famous for its setting and is dedicated to the archangel Saint Michael. They always go there to light candles when the sponge-fishing season has gone well. The island, he says, has very few trees, but the houses are beautiful—white, blue, and pink, with triangular pediments above the doors. The island isn't very rich, and many men emigrate. Then they come back and build these pretty houses.

"My sister will have the house and the land. We have a little land, with a few olive trees."

"What about you?"

"Look, we do what people on the island have always done. The girls: the house and the land. The boys: the boats, the nets, and the fishing tackle."

He promised that they'd invite me to his sister's wedding, too. They'll have a big party, like our Armenian parties, I suppose. But I've been worrying about a different problem. All this time it's been going around in my head: How could I come up with the money for diving equipment? Would my mother have to sell the only two pieces of jewelry she has left? Because now we were really poor. So I asked Iorgos. And he started laughing and told me not to worry at all, that his uncle will take care of it. "Promise me you won't think about it anymore! You have enough on your mind."

And then he added that it was nothing to be afraid of, but they had a whole extra outfit . . . that belonged to a sailor who'd died at sea, in an accident. Danger doesn't scare me anymore, and I won't lose any sleep tonight over the worries that used to keep me awake. Tomorrow I'll help my mother pack up the few things we have left for our trip to Marseille, which is coming up. There's lots of hustle and bustle these days among the groups sleeping at the opera because many of us are leaving. We'll catch up with Iorgos and his family later on, since they'll be selling coral there, and even set up a business if things go well.

My mother is sad again now that we're about to leave. She thinks we'll never go back home, or be able to bring flowers to Father's grave, wherever it is. I told her that wherever we go he'll be there, because we keep him in our memory.

"And there will be Armenia also," she replied, "because we carry it in our hearts."

But I don't dare talk to her about my sisters. Too often I heard her cry at night, in Etchmiadzin, when she thought I was sleeping.

I left "home" early this morning and spent the whole day with the gang from Symi, just as I'd planned with Iorgos. I tried on the helmet and the diving suit and started learning some of the signals. I already know them by heart; they're not hard. They're all with the rope, the guide rope, which they tied to my waist. For instance, one tug means:

"Attention! Are you alright?"

"I'm fine."

With two tugs I warn:

"Go back" or "Let out line."

Four tugs mean that I have to get out, they have to pull me up. I also learned how to do quick tugs. These quick signals are the most important: two quick tugs for "less air," three for "more air!"

They already let me go in the water, just below the surface. And today, on board, I tried on the lead-weighted boots. Going under didn't seem that strange to me, maybe because I'd already done so many dives, without gear, in the sea at home and in the Deguimen River.

My friends showed me the few tools we have to wear underwater: just a pouch that's attached with a kind of metal hoop, because that way it's always open and you don't lose time, and a pick to break up the coral. Coral fishermen, Iorgos told me, are the kings of divers, since we don't work with heavy tools like crowbars, pickaxes, or compressed air.

"My uncle," he also told me, "has already made arrangements with some Frenchmen and an Italian, from Livorno, who'll buy our coral. I'm excited to switch from sponge fishing to coral fishing. We'll begin near Port-Vendres and go down about midday."

"So you're leaving right away . . ."

"That's why I had you spend the whole day with us, Aram. We're leaving Piraeus the day after tomorrow. We already have the provisions and all the job things tied up. I'm sorry you're not coming with us!"

But I can't leave my mother alone, and I haven't even dared to ask her permission. Iorgos has thought of everything, and his uncle even more. I'll know where to look for them; they've given me a bunch of addresses in Marseille: a café at the port, the Greek church . . . and the Greek restaurant on the rue Longue-des-Capucins, the same street where we'll be living! It won't be hard for me to find them, once they're ashore.

Afterwards, Mr. Kontos, who knows everything about the port and what goes on there, showed me a white ship and told me that it's the ship that'll take us. It looks pretty old; they need to make a few repairs to it.

"But she's a good sailor!" he assured me. "Don't worry, she won't sink. I figure they'll let you board in about a week. Try and make yourself useful on board and earn some money. They always need deckhands."

I read the ship's name through his binoculars, because I can already read and understand Greek: *Samos*.

It goes without saying that Iorgos and his family invited me to eat with them. I was familiar with a lot of Greek delicacies from when we lived in Trebizond and my father's Greek friends, professors like him, invited us to parties. But after being so hungry in the mountains, and even hungrier in Etchmiadzin, and after the same food day after day in the refuge in Athens, everything tasted better. And especially eating on board, with the sea air, because the salt tang makes you hungry. And it's all great, the red mullet (*barbouni*, they call it), the octopus, which they know how to cook so well, and a delicious fish soup called *plaki*. Iorgos swore to me that outside of Symi and the other islands—the Dodecanese, his uncle clarified—they don't know how to make these dishes.

It was a farewell dinner, because tomorrow I have to go with my mother to the Near Eastern Relief dispensary, for her migraines, and afterwards they're leaving.

"Here, Aram, take good care of this."

They put a little bag in my hand and said there were some little sponges and shells inside, which I like.

"Don't open it until you're with your mother."

When we opened it, we both began to cry, Maryk and I, because inside was a silver medal of the archangel Saint Michael and a handful of coins, which we sure could use. Mother sewed the little bag to her dress so she won't lose it on the long voyage that awaits us, or have it stolen. But the medal I hung around my neck, and I'm going to wear it forever and always think about my good friend.

IV
Aram's Diary: At Sea

Would you look down on a stranger?
May you, then, find yourselves cast
out! Far from your own, you will have
time to learn the price of exile.
Should a stranger fill you with gold
a thousand leagues from your love,
may all that gold turn to ashes!

NAHAPET KUCHAK, FIFTEENTH CENTURY

On Board the *Samos,* from Corinth

I haven't been able to write at all until today because of
the work, the noise, and the novelty of the trip. We left
Piraeus at six in the morning, two days ago, and first we
went to a beautiful island (I don't remember the name,
one of the Cyclades) to pick up a group of children.
Because they'd gathered some seven thousand orphans
on this island, but it turns out they weren't all orphans,
and now we're taking the children who have a mother
or some other family member to France. Little by little,
all the ones who can will leave, as the Red Cross and

the NER fund find accommodation for them, because
Greece is poor.

Many of the children were crying and didn't want to
be separated from the *kyria*, the woman watching over
them, but in the end a kind nurse managed to convince
them, and now they've calmed down and are playing on
board. When we were in the Cyclades we saw a pod of
dolphins.

We stopped at Corinth. Because the *Samos* isn't very
big, it was able to pass through this narrow, rock-walled
canal, and that saved us a lot of time. As Mr. Kontos had
advised me to do, I offered to work, and I'm earning a
little money. But what I always get is mopping the deck,
helping to tie down the cargo, washing plates and glasses
in the kitchen . . . But, since I never get seasick, it's not
too hard to do.

I'll take advantage of the short breaks in the evening
to write, while my mother helps the nurse tuck the children in and get them to sleep.

On Board the *Samos,* at Sea

We stopped at Patras so the sailors could take advantage
of the trip by picking up a small load of those delicious
raisins they call "Corinth raisins," though they really
come from Patras. There are lots of vineyards around
the city. A little later on, an old sailor, Vasili, who's in
charge of me, told me to take a break for a while, and
he showed me the island of Ithaca, the island of Ulysses,

because we passed close by it. I know the story of Ulysses, *The Odyssey*, because my father told it to me when I was little, adventure by adventure, and more than once. My grandmother was likely to tell me the lives of the saints, like Joseph and his brothers, or Saint Mesrop, but Father talked about Hector and Ulysses.

"When you're older," he said, "if all goes well, we'll take a trip to Greece."

But everything has gone wrong, and my father will never go with me again, to Greece or anywhere else, and I can never swim in the Deguimen River again, either.

"Take a look, Aram," Vasili shows me. "We're passing by the Ionian islands."

"Aren't we going to stop at any of them?" I asked him.

And he explained that, no, we have to keep sailing to Brindisi, not too far away, to drop off a group who have relatives in Italy.

Then I thought again of my father, because he, too, stopped off at Patras and went to Corfu when he was very young, on his way to study in Venice. Vasili explained that if we hadn't had to drop off a group of emigrants who have family in Bari, we wouldn't have sailed this far north. After Patras we would've taken the route that goes between Italy and Sicily. But even with the rough seas I was glad to see Ithaca and to travel a little more of the same sea as Father had. Afterwards, our route won't be the same as his, because they, I seem to remember—he told it so well!—had sailed the Adriatic. Vasili confirmed as much: they must have gone straight from Corfu to Venice, unless they stopped on the Dalmatian coast.

The sea is starting to rock, and Vasili has sent me below deck. I was thinking that Maryk and I are living our own kind of odyssey, but the dangers have come not from monsters like the Cyclops or the bewitching sirens, but from men, who are supposed to be human like us.

I'll stop writing for today, or at least until we get to Brindisi, because the ship is shuddering too much, and I don't think I could read my own writing. There are some very strong gusts, but I'm not scared. Mr. Kontos told me the *Samos* is a good sail and very safe.

On Board the *Samos,* from Brindisi

Halfway between Patras and Brindisi we hit bad weather. I mean the wind was blowing really hard, and we pitched around a lot. Mother and a lot of other people got seasick, and almost none of them had any appetite. But I'm holding up well. If Iorgos had seen me, or my father, they'd have been proud. In Brindisi they dropped off a few families, who're staying with relatives in Italy.

Something strange is happening to me. When we were still in Greek waters, closer to the homeland that the evil Turks have taken, it was hard for me to write about our sufferings and adventures. But now that I'm in Italy and our destination is getting closer, I feel like I have to remember, because afterwards I'll have other obligations and new friends and maybe I'll forget a lot of things. Right now it seems impossible to forget them. They're burned into my thoughts like brands into the hides of cattle in the pastures of Van. And I don't want them forgotten, in case the day of vengeance arrives.

Mother's cousin, Grigor, didn't live in the city; he lived outside a village by the shores of a lake and was a farmer and shepherd. As soon as we'd kept my mother's promise and lit two candles and prayed at the ancient monastery of Narek and gone to mass, we went to his house. A man took us there in a cart pulled by a beautiful mare. It seems like we'd just gotten settled when the first news began to arrive. It was disturbing: war had broken out, then people were fleeing. Later it was hair-raising: men and women, their eyes staring or vacant, like ghosts, who couldn't say anything that made sense or fend for themselves, were staggering around like wounded birds. At night the adults would talk, and they'd send us out of the kitchen and exchange secrets. Sometimes I heard a few words if I listened in hiding:

"Russian soldiers . . . they'll save us . . . leave . . ."

A few days before seeing these terrified people, I noticed that Mother and her cousin were busier than usual, making strange preparations. Instead of cooking the good meals we'd had the first few days, food I hadn't eaten in Trebizond, they were making a lot of dough. But they were making not big loaves but a kind of flatbread. Mother explained that it was unleavened bread, and she didn't mind us kids helping her knead it and watch how it was cooked. They didn't bake it; they put it in a brick-walled pit in the ground that is heated by fire, and it was fun because it browns right away. Then they folded it just like we fold towels at home. They made a pile of it. This bread is called *lavash*, and we were really lucky to have it on the road, because you just wet it a little, and it's as good as the first day.

Grigor killed a couple of lambs, and he let us kids eat a few ribs. The rest he salted and smoked; I thought they were preserving it for winter. It was one more mystery I couldn't understand. I asked Mother:

"Why has Uncle Grigor killed two lambs all of a sudden?"

"You'll see soon, when it's time," she answered. "Go play, while you can."

When I realized something big was going to happen, though, something terrible, was the evening before we left—we didn't know we had to leave—because my cousin let all the farm animals loose in the meadow: lambs, sheep, calves, all of them. And that night they cooked us a delicious supper, and I realized that my mother and Grigor's wife were crying silently, drying their tears with the corner of their aprons. After supper, the adults stayed up for a long time, like the days before.

A few times us kids would hide behind the door, but they were talking softly, and we didn't know what they were planning. Later on I realized they didn't want to scare me and Gabriel; the little girl was too small to understand anything. And so the day after the animals were sent away, they called us early in the morning. Well, it was still dark out, even though it was summer, so it must have been before four, and they said:

"We have to go, boys. The Turks are coming, and they're killing all the Armenians. We have to go to the city of Van, and from there we can walk to Russian Armenia and we'll be safe."

Gabriel and I wanted to take some toys, of the few he had, but Grigor said:

"It's too late, Gabriel! Here, take this bundle of clothes and climb up on the cart! We'll eat breakfast on the way."

The truth is that they had to force my mother to go, because she didn't want to leave and she was screaming:

"I'll never see my loved ones again!"

For days, all Maryk had thought about was Father and Grandmother and the girls. We didn't know anything about them, and she was scared. Grigor's wife helped her into the cart and said:

"Maybe you'll hear something in Van."

Because our group, the ones on the pilgrimage, I mean, were going to stay in a convent in Van, to rest and gather our strength for the return journey—a journey that never happened. She added that my mother had to think about me and about them, and not put us all in danger. My little cousin was sleeping, Grigor had the two horses ready, and in the cart there were big bags of food and sacks, and I saw our suitcases, just two small ones, and two goats for milk, for my little cousin.

My cousins left everything behind: house, fields, flocks, fruit trees, tools, and we set out for the main road to Van. And when we got there we started seeing other refugees—some alone, others in groups, on foot, on horseback, in carts, and even some who crossed Lake Van by boat. At first it was cold, because Van is so high up, but later we suffered from heat and thirst, and many people got sick and even died, and we had to leave the ones that lagged behind.

I've forgotten a lot of these things. I wanted to forget them on purpose, in order to live. My mother often says, "When we left Van you were a child, and when we got to Etchmiadzin you were a young man."

It had been only a month and a half, I think, though the days seemed endless, but it means that I grew up overnight, like it or not. And I feel like it didn't happen during that whole time, but on the very day, the very morning, we arrived in Van. I'm sure of it, and it went the way I'll tell it here.

Grigor, my cousin, and I were on foot; from time to time, my mother made me climb up on the cart, and she would walk for a while. Grigor was leading a horse, and he often let me ride it, because it was a one-horse cart, and that way they didn't get so tired. Once, when I was walking, we saw a woman half-lying by the side of the road. And she held out a little baby and said breathlessly:

"Take the baby. I can't go on."

And I took the baby. But Grigor and Maryk, who understood the situation, got the woman into the cart. Before we got to the city, she'd died in my mother's arms. And I thought, who knows where she came from and what terrible things she must have seen. You could say I shed my childhood then and there.

On Board the *Samos,* from Genoa

We had smooth sailing all the way to the port of Genoa. We arrived at night, and it was the most beautiful thing I've ever seen. From the ship, because I'd gone up on deck, I could see thousands of specks of light—so many that it seemed like the stars had come down from the sky to the shores of Genoa. The sailors, except for the ones who were on watch, went down to the city to have a good time. They were in a good mood, but they didn't let any of us Armenians go with them, naturally, and the Red Cross nurses stayed on board, too, to take care of the sick and the children we'd picked up, because the littlest ones often wake up in the night and cry.

Now I want to write down some memories of our escape, even if I won't have much time, because they just served us supper, and I'll have to go to sleep soon. I don't have much light in the dining room, either.

Our group had met up with all the refugees who'd made it to the city of Van. Armenian and Russian soldiers were leading us. I learned afterwards that brave regiments of the Russian army were defending our rear, fighting constantly with the Turks and Kurds who wanted to kill us all. Commandants Keri and Hamazasp led these cavalry regiments.

Grigor, who's a very independent man, tried to get us to the front, because with the cart we could move along faster, and he didn't want to get stuck behind. Now, don't think the road was safe, because sometimes there were sudden attacks from bands or tribes of Kurds, to rob us of the few things we had left. And one night, listen to what happened, I'll remember it till the day I die, because if it hadn't been for me I don't know how things would have turned out.

We were getting closer to our destination, and we were passing along the foot of a mountain on a cloudy evening. We camped—if you can call it that—when it was already nighttime and dark. My uncle always unharnessed the horses and tied them to a tree, if there was one, or to the cart with a rope. The women and children were sleeping in the cart, and we were under the stars on a blanket. One or another of us almost always kept watch, because we never felt safe. But Gabriel and I often fell asleep, and my uncle didn't scold us.

So while it was still night, I woke up and heard a strange noise, and I called to Uncle Grigor:

"Uncle, Uncle! I think somebody's coming!"

We'd gotten a little too far from the group, because of my uncle's independent streak. And he said:

"Run like the wind and warn the soldiers!"

And I, all alone, stumbling, falling down, and getting up again, called to the soldiers, who were pretty far away. Too far, really. We were in time to save ourselves, but my uncle was wounded in one arm. In the weak light of dawn we made out some hateful shadows that were getting away . . . with our horses! What a disaster! Grigor had faced them down, and while he was protecting his chest, they wounded him in the arm—he didn't know if it was with a bayonet or a knife. One of the Russian soldiers, who knew something about wounds, dressed and disinfected the arm as best he could, and it healed, because Uncle Grigor was strong as an ox. My mother hugged me and said I'd saved everybody, thanks to my legs.

But, of course, we had to leave almost everything behind: the cart, lots of clothes, the suitcases, which were hard to carry. It goes without saying that the goats escaped in the uproar, or maybe the Kurds had taken them, too. My mother and Irina bundled up the food in blankets, which we would need in the winter, and even then, because the nights were cold. Maryk was carrying the little boy we'd saved, and Irina was carrying her own daughter. Even with his wound, Grigor strapped a bundle to his back and gave the other two to me and Gabriel. They were light: we hadn't saved much, and we shared the last lavash and a little salted meat, in little bites. The grownups ate only lavash.

"We can't give up," my mother said. "Come on, it's only a few days to Etchmiadzin."

Everyone said this word as if it were magic. A harbor. A safe haven. Many died along the way with this word on their lips. It was like we could feel it near, the refuge. But Irina, more and more tired and despairing, couldn't make it. One night she wouldn't even eat a last piece of lavash. "I'm not hungry," she said. "I don't feel well."

She lay down, wrapped in a blanket, and never woke up again. Her husband didn't want to leave her, like so many others, alongside the road, and before dawn he buried her. We all helped, digging at the dewy earth with knives and our swollen hands. My mother was praying and crying, and I carried Irina's little girl in my arms from that day on until we reached—how, I wouldn't be able to tell you—Etchmiadzin.

V

Maryk: Marseille

Red Earth

    I have here, on my table,
    a bit of soil from Armenia.
    The friend who gave it to me thought
    he was offering me his heart—without imagining
    that he was giving me that of his grandparents, too.
    I can't look away—as if my eyes were rooted.
    Red earth. I wonder: Where does this red come from?
    But, drinking of both life and sun,
    sucking from all the wounds,
    it was forced to turn red.
    The color of blood, I think,
    red earth, certainly, for it is Armenia!
    Perhaps the vestiges of millennial fires
    still breathe there, the glimmer of the snails
    that covered with red-hot dust
    the armies of Armenia . . .
    Perhaps there remains a bit of the seed
    that gave me life, a reflection of the
    dawn to which I owe this dark gaze,
    this heart in which beats a fire sprung
    from the very source of the Euphrates,

this heart that harbors both love and rebellion . . .

. . .

Red earth, exiled—heritage, relic,
offering, charm—just when a poem
trembles under my pen, I often weep
seeing this wretched bit
of Armenia, I howl—holding the soul
inside my hand,
I make a fist!

DANIEL VAROUJAN

Before he left with the Kontos clan, Aram gave me the little notebook where he writes about the trials of our family, and also things about his new perceptions.

"Here, Mother. Now I won't have time to write. You can continue if you want, Maryk."

Because he calls me Maryk as often as he calls me Mother, now that Vahe and the girls and my mother are gone. Boys usually keep what they write to themselves, but Aram and I trust each other completely now. Who else, what else, do we have, if they've taken everything from us?

I've read all that he's written so far: in Greece and on board the *Samos*, and I thought, Yes, I have to write, I can't leave our family's history hanging. People are so forgetful of the misfortunes of others! Now I don't write as well as my son. I haven't picked up a pen for a long time—and I used to like writing. I remember when I would write long letters to my cousin Irina—God rest her soul—and she would reply with just a postcard. In the evenings I'm tired from sewing—well, I'm lucky to have work—but I've decided to fill in the aching holes that Aram left empty. I think that later he can take up the thread when he returns from his time at sea, God willing.

I was impressed with Aram's insightfulness when he said that he grew up overnight when he took the infant from the arms of its dying mother. But I think that he'd begun to grow up in the days before that, on the trail of tears that was our desperate way from Armenia to Russia. Proof of that: from the beginning we rationed food, even though we had the two lambs, and not once did he ever ask for more or say he was hungry. And if it took a long time to get to a spring, and we were lucky enough to find one and fill all kinds of containers with water, he didn't let on that he was thirsty. Grigor let the boys drink wine, to give them strength, and not once did Aram ask for more. Gabriel did once in a while, but he, too, acted like a big boy, not like the child he was.

Many people from the city of Van had left without any provisions, but no one could give them any—we barely had enough for ourselves. There were days towards the end when we saw many people around us literally fall to the ground, but we kept on, without stopping, because we could hear the sound of the Turkish cavalry, or the howls of the enemies who were trying to cut off our retreat. Would they never have enough Armenian blood?

And we still thought, in moments of rest, at night, that if Aram and I hadn't gone to Van, we'd all be dead, drowned in the Black Sea. Because it's true that my vow saved us, Aram and me. I'd made the vow because the boy's health, with the pneumonia, had scared us to death. It's true that I meant to honor the vow when I made it. But it's true, too, that Vahe let us go because he thought the air of Van, with its mountains and forests, would be good for Aram. Neither he nor I could imagine the brutality that was drawing near: the shameful murder of all the Armenians in Turkey, from the Black Sea to Cilicia. We'd forgotten too soon the massacres of 1909.

So far had we forgotten them that the last word on Vahe's lips, when we said goodbye, was *roses*.

To start with, I want to write down a few things about the life of Vahe, my beloved, unforgettable husband. Vahe was a poet in love with Armenia, and he transmitted his passion to me. I know many of his poems by heart: I recite them to myself when I can't fall asleep at night. Vahe's father was a doctor. Luckily for him, he and his wife died of sickness before the catastrophe.

"I'll always be grateful to my father," my husband used to say, "for sending me to Venice, to study with the Mekhitarist fathers on the island of San Lazzaro."

Because the Mekhitarist monks of San Lazzaro have guarded the treasures of our culture. Afterwards, Vahe finished his studies at the University of Ghent. I often think that if Vahe hadn't come back, he would have escaped death. But he loved Armenia too much to ever resign himself to living in exile from our country. Aram always says that one way or another Vahe must have joined the rebels at Musa Dagh, to die fighting. But I'm not sure, and I have a terrible presentiment about his death.

The girls! My flowers, our treasures, their warm, soft bodies, their beautiful eyes . . . And Grandmother, she must have held the two of them close until the last swallow of bitter water that drowned them. My little ones, who would beg me before falling asleep, "Sing us the song, Mama."

The same lullaby that I'd learned from my mother:

> Sleep, my child, and close your eyes.
> Let your pretty eyes grow drowsy.
> Sleep and make me sleepy, too,
> Mother of God, bring him slumber.
> Lu-lu, my son, lu-lu, lullaby.
> Now the baby is falling asleep.

Other times they wanted the one about the apple tree. "Today it's the apple tree!"

> Under the apple tree,
> I loved you, my dear,
> under the apple tree.
> Welcome, beloved,
> with your red sandals.

Grandmother sang songs to them, too; she adored the little ones. Aram, too, of course, but he, she'd tell me, "is growing away from me." When Sofia was born, she wouldn't leave her side. She was the one who noticed that her first tooth was coming in, from her red gums. So, as is our custom, it was she who prepared the sweets when, on Sunday, we invited relatives and friends to celebrate the first tooth. She prepared the flour with such excitement, mixing in the raisins, walnuts, hazelnuts, and sweet almonds. She didn't skimp on the sugar or the candied fruit or the red pomegranates, so carefully seeded and cleaned.

She got so much pleasure from it that when Yaneh's first tooth broke through, and this time I'd seen it first, I pretended I hadn't seen it so that Grandmother could enjoy the discovery. How the memory of these little pleasures comes to mind, now that the girls' mouths are closed forever! I even remember that my mother said, "Maryk, my eyes are better than yours! I can see a little white line in the baby's gums!"

And so she had the privilege of making the *hadig* again. According to her, no baby had ever cut their first teeth as early as our little girls. Every step they took growing up was a wonder, never to be repeated. Such was her love for Sofia and Yaneh, who were only a year and a half apart. The truth is that she helped me so much to bring them up.

She'd sewed their little sheets, and we baptized our three children in my christening dress, which she had embroidered and trimmed with lace with her own hands. How could I ever forget their grandmother? And all the times she stayed by their cradle so Vahe and I could go out?

What a different kind of cradle, the bitter sea! For the little ones, for the mother who had rocked me to sleep. Yes, I have to write it down: there was no mercy for either the old people or the infants, all the children, all the women, herded onto ships and drowned in the Black

Sea, cold-bloodedly. We learned of this some time after arriving at Etchmiadzin, from the NER and the Red Cross. For years I cried for them at night so as not to sadden Aram. One night, when we were in Athens, an older woman who was sleeping nearby heard me:

"Why are you crying, Maryk?"

"For my little girls and their grandmother. I told you how they died."

"You don't have to cry for them," she said, almost coldly. "They were little, they died right away."

"And what do you mean by that?"

"I had two grown granddaughters, sixteen and seventeen. My son lived far from us, in Bitlis."

"And what happened to them?"

"The Turks, may God confound them, killed all the men and carried off and raped the girls and the pretty women. Some of them they sold. My granddaughters were beautiful: now they're in the hands of the blasted Turks, who knows where! That's why I say you don't have to cry for yours."

I know, perhaps, where the girls are buried: the tide, someone told me, carried the bodies to shore, under the walls of the Italian monastery near the beach, and the Greek women buried all the bodies the waves brought in. May God bless them.

It's very easy, when the horrors are over, to look back and say:

ARAM'S NOTEBOOK

"How did you not realize there was trouble? Didn't you remember the massacres at Adana?"

But when your life is quiet, filled with everyday affairs, when the sun rises over the sea and the streets and the ones you love, you don't have an inkling of anything bad. Very few of us did, and no one could imagine Turkish cruelty would go so far. No one. And it's only been since we've lived in Marseille, and we're among our own, the Armenians—some from Bitlis, some from around Van, a few who escaped from Musa Dagh or were rescued by French ships near Syria—and we get together and talk after church, that we've found out more details. Incredible, as sharp as the bayonets driven into the chests of our men by the criminal Turks. Maybe into Vahe's, who knows, my God?

I see that Aram recalls certain episodes of our flight. He remembers them separately. It seems to me that he wanted to forget the time we spent in eastern Armenia, in Etchmiadzin and Yerevan, because it was very hard for a boy, almost a child in age. Children without a childhood, by the thousands. For my part, I remember everything. I'd be glad to bury many memories deep inside my brain, where forgotten things end up. I'd like to bury them like seeds in the red earth, but I can't. The happy times, the years in Trebizond, are behind us, like the golden coins of a lost treasure. At least I have Vahe's poems, a part of him. Many times I put his books under my pillow at night. I don't ever want to forget him. I cannot forgive.

I don't want to go on about how we got to Etchmiadzin. I wouldn't know how to describe it. Vahe would've known, or his Dante. Now these events are known, after the reports from the British and the College of Physicians, as well as the foreign missionaries. Many unfortunate refugees died from hunger, from exhaustion, from sickness. But we had hope that we were going towards a safe haven, towards life. It was in Athens and Marseille that we found out that thousands of other Armenians were walking towards death, led by their executioners and not, like us, by friendly soldiers. We could drink whenever we found rivers or springs, we had clothes to cover us at night, no one beat us. But those who were deported to the desert weren't allowed to drink, or stop at a spring, or eat. The girls were taken off and raped, and those who lagged behind were flogged with whips or rifles.

Somehow, five of our little group of six survived, including the little one Aram took from the arms of its mother. We were able to revive him, and Aram carried him. As soon as we got to Etchmiadzin, the city of the Catholicos, once we'd recovered some strength, resting on the ground, we took him to the hospital they'd set up, along with my cousin's little girl, who'd come down with scarlet fever. The nurses took them in right away, and we left them there. We couldn't do anything for them ourselves; we couldn't help; we had no food or medicine, or even a house, or anything. I've never seen them again. May the Mother of God watch over them, the hope of the hopeless.

The last days of our escape through the mountains were the most wretched of all, since by then they'd stolen our horses. My cousin died just before we found shelter. Did she die of exhaustion, or from grief? I'm not really sure. All I know is that she was a victim of the Turks.

My case was different. In Trebizond we had a more eventful life than hers. I mean that we'd gone to other cities, on trips; we'd spent some time at sea. And, of course, Vahe had lived abroad. But Irina was rooted to her land like a tree; to transplant her was to kill her. She was truly the mistress of those lands; her parents are buried in the cemetery in Van. Her whole world was the house and the fields, the trees she could see from the flowered window of her dining room. I think she started dying the day before we left, when her husband sent the animals away so it would be hard for the Turks and Kurds to take them. When she lost sight of the rows of trees they'd planted when their son and daughter were born, so they'd have wood, one day, to build their own houses. But there would be neither houses nor future, she must have thought, as the trees faded from view: the tall, leafy ones planted for Gabriel, and the tender saplings that marked the birth of her little girl.

That is the sickness that burrowed into Irina's heart and soul: the loss of her whole, warm world, worked by her own hands, as by the hands of her great-grandparents: the pastures, the gentle animals, the sheep that gave them wool, the sheep that she milked, the wool that she spun with her own tireless hands—hands that also made butter, took bread from the oven, rocked her children in the old wooden cradle.

Not that Grigor and Gabriel weren't pained by all of this, but they were stronger. My cousin had become a little delicate after giving birth to her second child and caring for her. Gabriel wasn't thinking about the house and the land; like the child he still was, he was more sorry about leaving his dog. Not the older dog that went off with the flock, but a puppy. In fact, he hid it and took it with him, but Grigor told him:

"We can't take him, it's a long trip. Send him off, let him go."

So Gabriel let him go, but the dog came back, in the flood of refugees, and jumped into the cart. Grigor said that he'd have to kill him in the end, because they couldn't spare him any food, and then my nephew, who was bright as a button, ran over to the soldiers. And they took pity on him, they were touched by him, and they kept the dog with the regiment. Maybe the dog even survived, but sweet Irina did not. And we were even able to bury her, because at the time we were passing through an area that wasn't too rocky. Others, hundreds of them, were abandoned to the birds of prey by the side of the road.

We weren't in Etchmiadzin for very long. There were too many of us for such a small city, though some good-hearted folk from the village of Igdir had begun to collect food and clothes for the refugees. All those of us from

Van were on the verge of exhaustion, since we'd come by way of Persia. Afterwards I learned that there were some fifty thousand of us. More than double that had walked through the plains of Abagha, and the Armenian regiments under Andranik and Dro had helped the Russian general protect us. There were too many of us, as I said; we could find neither bread nor a place to sleep. And though they'd tried—the Patriarch and the doctors and the refugee committee—to control the avalanche, it was impossible. Luckily some volunteers arrived from Tiflis and from Armenian organizations in Moscow and Baku, as we learned. But the sick and the orphans nullified all their efforts because of the epidemics.

Very early, Grigor understood the situation and told me:

"We have to go to Yerevan before winter comes."

It was the month of September when he decided, and he was absolutely right. Because in summer we could get by sleeping under a tarp, but how would we survive the cold? We had no defenses against it, our bodies had become weak. The boys were so thin you could see their ribs under their tattered clothes. We lived on roots and cresses, on berries and unripe fruit, which Grigor knew how to find in the fields and woods, on apples from trees growing wild. No one wanted our Turkish money, or they'd give us next to nothing for it. I wanted to sell the jewelry I'd carried since Trebizond, but my cousin told me to wait and do it in Yerevan, if we could get there. I doubted we'd make it because I saw so many sick and dead all around us. Suffice it to say that they had to expand the cemetery to hold all the victims. They had to bury them in mass graves and cover them with lime because of the epidemics, and once a week they'd hold a service for all of them. I heard afterwards from the NER that there were a few days when the death count reached almost a hundred.

But, luckily, trains finally arrived carrying flour, sugar, tea, and all kinds of clothing. Our Armenian brothers and sisters to the north, from Moscow and other cities in Russia, had sent them. There was enough for everybody! So we could eat lots of bread, as much as we wanted, and drink cup after cup of sweet tea, which gave us our strength back.

So we managed to walk to Yerevan, which wasn't too far. It's a beautiful city, full of fountains, from which you can always see the snowcapped peak of our holy mountain, Ararat. Grigor, who's very sharp, realized that with so many refugees and only so much flour, the bakers wouldn't be able to keep up with demand. So he started looking everywhere for work baking, which he knew how to do. I should say that by then we had a roof over our heads, the coming of winter didn't frighten me as much, and I didn't experience the shortening of the days with as much anguish as when we were in Etchmiadzin.

He and I had sold the jewels, Irina's and mine. All I had left was my wedding ring and earrings. With this we could rent a ground-floor flat—a single room and a kitchen—and buy a little firewood for the winter. There were only four of us, since Grigor's little girl and the baby were in the orphanage in Etchmiadzin.

We lived on bread, bread soup, and tea with lots of sugar—nothing else. But one day Grigor managed to find a job; he got it from a baker who was up to his ears in work now that all the refugees had ration tickets and the committee was paying. So he hired my cousin and his son, just for food, no pay. But the food was plentiful and very good, which they deserved for the number of hours they worked, and almost every day he managed to bring "home" a plate of something. One day he brought us *kufta*, and other times mutton cooked with vegetables, which was a real treat, or great soups with barley and yogurt. We had enough for supper, and I even kept sauce for the next day, to put in Aram's soup.

Then I began sleeping a bit better, because in the early days, between the hunger and the memories, there were nights I could barely close my eyes. For a long time I had frequent dreams about that long, painful march, and I'd wake up with my heart beating a mile a minute. During the day I tried not to think about it, and I mostly remembered Vahe, the girls, and their grandmother. But at night I again saw bodies lying by the side of the road, like so many we'd had to leave, little children, old people. Or else I would dream that a band of Kurds was after us and I was trying to run and my legs wouldn't work, and they were about to catch me. Then I'd wake up, and in the midst of so much sorrow I'd experience a feeling of relief. One night I found myself—as real as the day it happened—helping a woman from Van give birth. Irina and I were assisting, especially Irina, who knew more, because it wasn't the first time for her. It was before they'd taken our cart, and we took in that poor woman, who was on foot and would stop from time to time and cry out. So we pulled her into the cart, but we couldn't stop because they were always after us. And that's how she had her child, without stopping. The cart was rocking back and forth on the road, and it was hard to stop the bleeding, but Irina did it. I think I dreamt about that, and the newborn's cries, more than once, and I think I know why.

Our situation got worse and worse. The provisions were running out. That's why we couldn't be compassionate, not as much as we would have liked, with our comrades in flight. We had three children, and we had to look out for them. Well, to come right out with it, we only took care of the woman and her little one for two more days. Then we gave her a few pieces of flatbread, we filled her jug with milk, and, without a word being said, she realized we were saying goodbye. I think that's why I dreamt about her, until one day I saw her in the bread line in Etchmiadzin. They'd survived! After that the dream became less frequent.

Little by little we got used to our new life in Yerevan. Well, we had to. With all this, many months had passed since our horrible flight, and the boys had recovered. The food Grigor brought home from the bakery had been a blessing for us all.

It seemed, too, that he'd gotten over the death of our Irina, whom I dearly missed. So much so that when he came home from work, after lunch, he would hug me too tightly for a cousin. Until one day he said:

"Now that the boys are out, we have to talk."

The truth is we had little time for talking. They left to go to the bakery at four or five in the morning, and in the afternoon Grigor slept for a while. He worked a lot and came home tired, more tired than Gabriel. He needed to nap. I made sure the boys didn't make noise so he could rest. The day before holidays he often had to go back to work in the afternoon. But one day he didn't lie down, and he sent the boys outside, cold as it was, though perhaps Gabriel would rather have gotten some rest, which he sometimes needed.

"What is it, Grigor?"

I was afraid there was some bad news. Maybe he had to tell me he'd lost his job. But it had nothing to do with that.

"Maryk, you are fond of me, right? Am I wrong to think that?"

"I love you very much, of course. You've been like a brother to us, like a father."

"Maryk, I don't need a sister. I need a woman, a real woman."

Then he told me that his boss had offered to lodge him at his house. There was room, and they'd be nice and warm. He was sure he could get the offer extended to me and Aram, he said. We could be together, and later on, when we had official confirmation of Vahe's death, we could have a church wedding.

"Because you shouldn't fool yourself, Maryk. They've surely killed him."

I was shocked, though I could surely have expected such a proposal. I didn't want to live with Grigor unmarried, or to be his wife either. He was so different from my Vahe! But neither was I ready to stay in Yerevan forever with Aram. So I told my cousin, as best I could, that I couldn't be with him, that I still wanted to wait for news of my husband.

"Fine, Maryk, I won't force you. I'll find some other woman, as many as I want, who'll be more grateful . . ."

I started crying because I felt frightened, all alone. But he told me to calm down, that we wouldn't ever stop being friends and family. I would never be without bread.

"But how will we manage, Aram and I?"

"Look, you have the rent paid for three months. After that you'll have to look for something. The Brotherly Aid won't abandon you, and every Sunday I'll bring you bread for the week."

In fact Grigor was able to choose a young woman, a countrywoman from close to Van, and Aram and I were left on our own. The end of the three months was approaching, and I'd found no solution, no work. We were living again on bread, bread soup, and tea. I skimped on firewood so it would last, but Aram caught a bad cold, with a cough and fever. So I took him to the Brotherly Aid's dispensary, where we had to wait in line for a long time. And when they called us in, the doctor who saw my son kept staring at him. And as he asked the nurse for some medicine, he kept on staring at him and said:

"This boy looks just like a friend of mine."

And he insisted, in a loud voice:

"This boy is the spitting image of Vahe!"

"Doctor, my husband is named Vahe, he studied in Venice."

"Say no more! I was there, too. So you're Vahe's widow? The widow of our poet?"

Widow . . . Vahe. Words like hammer blows, with the ring of steel. They'd killed Vahe. A black cloud covered my eyes. I sat down on a chair. I heard his voice as if from far away.

"Good Lord, Hripsimé, she's about to faint! Rub her wrists with alcohol, give her some air."

And a few moments later he brought me a glass of cognac and asked if I didn't know that my husband was dead, that he was on the endless list of the dead. He'd heard it from the College of Physicians. All the Armenian doctors, clergymen, and professors in Trebizond, he told me, had been killed by the Turks. How, he didn't know. He'd studied with Vahe at Saint Mekhitar on the island of San Lazzaro and was a passionate admirer of his poetry. He made me promise to bring Aram back the next day. He wanted to keep an eye on his illness.

But that wasn't the real reason he wanted us to come back. Truly, I wouldn't have guessed it even in my wildest dreams. I realized that he'd wanted to talk with his family, because the next day he offered us lodging and anything else we needed. He had a big house, he assured me, and he couldn't allow the poet's widow and his son to go without. So we packed up our things—which were fewer each time—and moved into the doctor's house. He was a lovely person.

His wife was waiting for us with a warm smile, and she took us to a big bedroom with two beds, two armchairs, and a beautiful icon on the wall. When she shut the door and told us to rest for a while, that she'd call us for supper, I got down on my knees before the icon. It was the Mother of God who heals all wounds. I couldn't believe it. We had a roof over our heads once again, a warm house to protect us. After supper, the doctor's wife gave me one of her dresses, which just needed to be taken in, and a black coat. She also gave my son some clothes from her older boy.

I didn't want to be a bother or a parasite in that house. So I offered to work, and there was certainly plenty to do. She had me mend and iron all the clothes, especially the white coats and the sheets from the clinic. As for Aram, the doctor enrolled him in the same school as his sons, and Aram studied hard.

So in our exile we found a period of calm, a warm respite, in Dr. Arshag's home. I'll never forget it. The war ripped it apart, without respite, without pity. The cursed Turks were advancing again, and the doctor went to the front to help the wounded. Provisions soon began to be scarce and expensive. We didn't lack for anything, but I realized that two extra mouths were becoming a burden. And, above all, even though the Armenians and Russians had won two important battles, I was terrified that our killers would make a comeback. I couldn't sleep at night with so many thoughts swirling in my head. I had to make a decision.

"Aram," I told him one night, "we have to go. We're beginning to be a burden on this family. We have to go far away from this war, far from the Turks. For good."

But Arshag's wife kept us at her house for some time, until the situation in Europe seemed more favorable for the long and difficult voyage that awaited us. The doctor, who was allowed to come home from time to time until the end of the war, helped us secure the paperwork for emigration, though unwillingly. We put our names on the Brotherly Aid's lists of Armenians waiting to go to France or America. In the meantime, Greece was willing to take us in, without conditions. There were ninety thousand of us. An English organization was paying travel expenses.

"Goodbye, red earth; goodbye, Armenia," I prayed when we lost sight of the snow on our sacred mountain. "Goodbye forever."

VI
Aram's Diary: Alexia

But, fearing to lose everything if I try to be
exhaustive, like eyes too weak to bear the
sight of the sun, I will say few things and
pass over many in silence.

GREGORY OF NAREK, TENTH CENTURY

*(I transcribe Aram's words and the translation of the
diary pages that he attached to the notebook. Aram's notes
are more infrequent now that he's working as a coral diver.)*

June 4, 1921—Marseille

It's been so long since I've written in this little notebook!
I hadn't gotten back to it since we got here, on board the
Samos. When I asked my mother for it and, after, when
I had it in my hands, I suddenly remembered that it was
my father who'd bought it for me. He gave it to me before
the pilgrimage to the monastery at Narek.

"Take this, Aram," he told me. "Here's a new notebook, so you can write about the new things that you'll
see on this long trip."

But instead of travel notes it's become a memoir about, mostly, the misfortunes of our people. There are a lot of facts missing, big and small, because it's always been with us in troubled times. But now we seem to be in a period of calm, and Mother has gotten quite used to Marseille. But I have a lot of work, I spend a lot of time at sea, and I'm not free to write much.

But today, or rather yesterday, was a very important day, and it occurred to me to return to the notebook. I'm happy to be able to set down this day in the little book that Father bought for me. I think every Armenian alive has been glued to the radio for the past two days, when we weren't at church praying for Soghomon Tehlirian. I'll bet that in every city and country where there are Armenians, joy broke out like it did here, in Marseille. Because there are so many of us, the happiness was delirious: shouting, singing, hugging, from streets to houses to factories. In Lyon, in Paris, in America, it must have been the same.

They've freed Soghomon Tehlirian! Our avenger, our heroic student, is free! He walks the streets!

Le Provençal

After a brief trial, the Berlin tribunal declared Sog-homon Tehlirian innocent of the murder of Talaat, ex–Minister of Interior Affairs of Turkey, and one of the principal organizers of the massacre, plun-der, and deportation of the Armenian people. We recall that Talaat, Shakir, Djemal, and Nazim had been tried in absentia and condemned to death for their crimes by a Turkish court-martial in the city of Constantinople.

We remind our readers as well that the tribunal did not try them until they were outside of the country, by way of Odessa and Germany; the defendants present in court were condemned to incarceration and briefly deported to the island of Malta. According to our sources, the Armenian Revolutionary Federation decided in secret to carry out the sentence. Soghomon Tehlirian was, then, an officer of the court, not an assassin. In other news, criminals accused of "minor" offenses and tried in other Turkish cities have been sentenced.

Mother and I have never gotten involved in politics— it was hard enough to survive. But we'd heard rumors that the most prominent Turkish murderers would be executed, since they'd escaped justice. Talaat had even changed his name and thought he could live peacefully in Berlin. The day they executed him I was at sea, I recall, but as soon as we were back to Marseille with the coral, everyone rushed to tell me: the shop owners around the port, who know me, the seamstresses, the factory workers, everyone was full of the news. Even the Der Baba, who sometimes preached forgiveness, was praying for Soghomon's freedom.

On Sunday we'll have a party to celebrate, a real Armenian party, and I'll be able to be there because we don't weigh anchor until Monday. It's all planning and high spirits, despite the memories that never leave us. It'd been a long time since we had a satisfaction like this. The choirs are practicing, led by the first cantor, and not only religious songs but hymns to the heroes, popular songs . . . We'll all take part. We've bought some fat young lambs, and, just like back in Armenia, we'll deck them out with ribbons and garlands of flowers, and after mass, because there'll be a meal for the whole congregation, we'll roast them outside.

And that's not all: Mother and a whole band of other women are toiling to make a huge amount of *mante*. One of the schools has lent them a kitchen, and they've raised the money to buy the meat to stuff the *mante*. They already have the yogurts ready for the sauce. We'll be licking our fingers!

Afterwards there will be dancing, too, and we'll hear Armenian music again. I've given Mother, who always wears black, a white silk shawl and convinced her to wear it to the party. At first, she was working for the celebration and didn't want to come to it! But we'll go together. Our dead are starting to be avenged.

Dear Maryk . . . how beautiful my mother looked today! You can tell that everyone in our "colony" loves her. Many women, little children, and grown men came to greet her and thank her for the favors she's done them. She sewed a dress for one woman's child; for another she deciphered some French documents, as many women still don't know how to read (the alphabet is so different from ours). For another family she took in a relative while the Brotherly Aid was looking for a place for them.

I had no idea that she had so, so many friends, because I'm at sea so much, but you could see it. Luckily she has more time now. I'm earning a living, I can help her, and with a few hours on the sewing machine she has enough. My friends from Symi, as well as other Greeks from Marseille, were invited to the party. Some of our bunch hadn't met Maryk, and afterwards they said:

"What a mother you have, Aram! She seems so kind and good!"

"And pretty," added Aris, who's always after the girls.

And it's true. Today, with the happiness of Tehlirian's liberation, her black eyes were sparkling. She even looked young to me; she still is, though the black braid wrapped around her head has gray in it now. She looked beautiful holding a bouquet of roses brought by a man she'd helped get a job at a factory.

Even Father Arshavir, the youngest priest, came to greet her. He's very pleased that we've finished the expansion of the Armenian church. Everyone helped, with their labor, or money, or whatever they could. He greeted me, too, when he came over to thank Mother for her work on the party.

"Your mother helps us so much with her kindness. She lets us know if there's someone in need among the Armenians, always with a smile."

His eyes seemed to be attracted to Maryk's face. I know that she volunteers at the parish. No other woman knows as much as she does about decorating the icons and the altar with flowers, and I would be surprised if she didn't often iron their robes and capes. Father Arshavir is tall and well groomed, and his beard is always trimmed. He has a lovely, deep, and melodic voice. He's an Armenian from Cilicia—one of the few clergymen who survived the massacres, because the Turks respected neither *babas* nor bishops and hung many of them in front of their own churches.

I think Father Arshavir would like to marry Maryk; I can tell from the attention he lavishes on her. And I would never object, if that were the case. With my job I have to leave her alone for whole days, whole weeks when we go down the Catalan coast. And Mother, I mustn't forget, is only thirty-eight years old.

But Maryk soon leaves Father Arshavir and chats with other people. I know Vahe is always on her mind, and the girls and Grandmother, though she doesn't talk to me about it as much as before. I believe she also misses our home in Trebizond and the rose garden. If our coral expeditions continue to go well, like this one, and I continue to get work at sea, soon we can rent a bigger apartment. I've always thought about a house with a garden, or a patio or a terrace, where she can have lots of roses. For now she makes do with a few planters on our little balcony. They aren't roses from Anatolia; they're from Provence.

April 18, 1922

Grandma and the Girls Have Been Avenged!

Le Provençal

Two of the Turkish politicians condemned to death have been shot: Shakir, a national leader; and Djemal Azmi, former *vali* of Trebizond, especially notorious for his cruelty. He was responsible for the deaths of thousands of Armenians, who were herded onto sailboats and drowned in the Black Sea.

A military court of appeal had reversed the sentences, but, as this paper has discovered, the Armenian Revolutionary Federation carried out the executions as an act of justice. Presumably the recent absolution of Tehlirian gave them new incentive. According to eyewitnesses, it was almost midnight when two Armenians sighted Shakir and Azmi in a group of men and women, all Turkish, near Azmi's residence. One of the Armenians pushed aside Talaat's wife, who had attempted to intervene, fired at Azmi, and took him down with one shot; his second shot wounded Shakir, who was then shot in the forehead by the second Armenian. Both were able to escape. There were no other deaths or injuries.

Of the central leadership of the former Turkish government—masterminds of the "Special Organization" dedicated to planning and carrying out the massacre of Armenians—the most important and visible survivors are now Djemal, Enver, and Nazim. Though not expressed publicly, the question on everyone's mind is: How long will it take for their fate to catch up with them?

Through the Red Cross we finally received a letter from my cousin Gabriel. Thanks to the initiative of a Norwegian doctor named Nansen, the NER has set up agricultural projects in eastern Armenia. Gabriel and Grigor are working there teaching agriculture to orphan boys who have finished school. So my cousins have become farmers and shepherds again, and they're happy about it. He writes that they live in a house. Grigor has remarried and brought the little one with them. His father's wife is kind and a very good cook. I'm truly glad they're well, because they helped us a lot. We may never see them again, but we'll write from time to time. For myself, I don't know if I could've gotten used to living so far inland, so far from the sea.

So I'm glad that Mother decided to emigrate to France, and to Marseille. It's right on the sea—from the church they call Notre-Dame de la Garde there's a view of the Mediterranean that I love. Some people tell me that my job as a coral diver is dangerous, but it doesn't seem that way to me. The real dangers I've faced have always been on dry land!

I compare the sea with the difficulties of our exodus, that terrible flight, and especially with all the killings and threats of the Turks, and, truly, I think that underwater is just fine. I've learned that men are more dangerous than sharks or eels. Below the surface the sea is calm; there's a silence and a peace that I love and that make me forget all the worries of home. I would've worked as a deck-hand if necessary, because I needed work, but it turns out that I'm a good diver.

I'm happy, too, that I haven't made Iorgos look bad, because he'd said so much about me to his family about my skill and love for the sea. I work with friends, especially my best friend Iorgos. What more could I ask? I'm like a member of the Kontos family. Yes, sometimes it's hard extracting coral from some deep cove, especially when there's wind on the surface, which clouds your vision; the deeper you go, the less you see. But I've gotten used to it. And, sometimes, if you're lucky and the day is clear with a southwest wind, the water is cleaner and you can see the fish. With practice, you could count every white flower on the coral when it blooms.

That's why I often tell Maryk's friends, Armenians from Van and from the interior, that men are far more fearsome than water or fish. Maybe I'm lucky, but no eel has ever attacked me, and dressed as we are in rubber, the jellyfish don't worry me. Because we have a good boss and trust the guide on deck, our job is no more danger-ous than any other. Iorgos feels the same.

At the beginning of the day, for fun, we sometimes take a dip bare-chested, just below the surface for only a few delicious moments, to see the colors of the fish and the luminosity of the water. In this upper layer we see all the pink, gray, and silvery fish. This is what we do when Kontos lets us, because he takes good care of me, as he promised my mother. Then, when we're working, it's another story. If we're lucky we see the coral from above, because the light quickly diminishes with the depth, and we ourselves make it cloudy by walking over the rocks and stirring up the bottom. So we can't let ourselves be distracted by anything.

Another advantage of our work is that, aside from the coral, one or the other of us always gets some fish. I'm always so hungry at meals that my coworkers make fun of me. But they don't know what it is to be really hungry! I don't want to think back on the herbs of Etchmiadzin when I sit down to a corvina, a sea bream, or even poor cod or grilled sardines and all the potatoes and wine I want, or a nice, Symi-style fish stew. We have a great cook!

August 8, 1922

(I don't know if you've noticed that Aram took note of the date only when writing or relating news about the killers of his people.)

Armenia, publication of the Armenians of Marseille

Two more of the accused from the proceedings in Constantinople have died. Djemal was unable to escape the hand of justice, though he had planned to find refuge in Georgia.

(Only two remained, therefore: Enver and Nazim. Before transcribing the note referring to Enver, I have to put it in its political context. Russia, and the republics that came to form the USSR, were shaken by constant wars, the Communist Revolution, and bloody civil wars during these years.)

> Enver had escaped justice by fleeing to Moscow and in 1921 securing a command in the Soviet army. But the Communists did not trust him and watched him closely. He then decided to flee to the mountains and join the "Bamajis," that is, the Muslims who called themselves "warriors of the true faith." Someone, however, followed his tracks. On August 4, the Bamaji camp was surrounded, and the troops under Enver's command annihilated. His body was later found because the Koran, signed in his name, allowed him to be identified. At this point, of those who escaped the sentence of their fellow Turks, only Nazim is still alive.

(Aram stopped writing before Dr. Nazim met his fate. Maryk, on the other hand, never made any reference to this matter in her own notes.)

1923

(It seems that Maryk and Aram now feel very much at home in their new city, Marseille. Aram's first diary entries, from Athens, were written when he was fifteen years old. I think I'm right, then, in saying that he was nineteen years old in 1923, because the Armenian refugees stayed in Greece for quite a long time.)

If my father saw me now—a real artisan, as Maryk calls me—he would be proud. For some time now I've accepted that he's dead, though we haven't been able to find out any details amid all the chaos. But maybe it won't be long before we find out more information, since we've received a letter from Paris, from the widow of another murdered poet. She surely got our address through the Red Cross, and she sent us a few lines saying that she shared our pain. She didn't say much more, but she has words of admiration for Vahe's poetry and says that, circumstances permitting, she'll come and see us in Marseille.

But today I'm writing for an even more important reason. I'm engaged! I'm engaged to the prettiest and most charming girl in the world . . . Iorgos's little sister, my Alexia! I know we're very young, and it'll be a while before we marry. And now we're far apart, she's in Symi, but none of that matters, since we're engaged for real. This I do have to explain!

I hadn't been able to go the island for the wedding of Iorgos's sister, but I did make it, along with the whole crew, to the baptism of her child. I accepted the invitation because the Italians are in charge of Symi now; if the blasted Turks had been in charge I wouldn't have gone anywhere near it. My friend's father is a fisherman; he fishes with his son-in-law. They live in a small but pleasant house near the port. It's pink and white, with bright red geraniums in the windows and along the front steps. They also have a patio, which is perfect for repairing their equipment. When Iorgos's father, Yanni, isn't fishing, he's at work mending his nets, because the dolphins and turtles and rocks often damage them.

I stayed with them for the week before and then the four days of Easter, and the following Tuesday we celebrated the baptism. The church of the Panagia (the Mother of God) where they baptized the little boy is very pretty, with beautiful silver oil lamps—though not as pretty as the monastery of Panormitis, which we visited as well. They took me there by boat. Yanni's boat is called *Dimitra*, and if my friend wants to go back to Symi one day, it'll be his. Right away, everyone treated me like one of the family, but I had eyes only for Alexia, charming and tall. When she looked at me with something between shyness and delight, I could see the whole world in her green eyes. Right away I could tell she liked me. When she served me food it seemed as if she gave me the best pieces, the choicest fish.

I think I fell in love right away, really. The first few days, and even on Good Friday or Saturday, I hardly dared to say a word to her. But on Sunday, between the joyful ringing of the bells and the preparations for the baptism, I worked up the courage, and when we went outside to see the fireworks at night, we separated from the group without a word and mixed with the crowd. While every-one else was watching the rockets and the sparklers, I put my hand on her wrist, first, and then on her slim waist. She didn't pull away, but I was too respectful—she was Iorgos's sister. It was she—my Alexia—who kissed me on the forehead when a burst of sound and light made me close my eyes!

"Alexia," I said, "would your family have me? Because Iorgos is my best friend, my brother. I don't want to play with you."

She burst out laughing.

"Me either, I'm not playing! I gave you a kiss because I like you. The house is full of people these days," she added. "I'll wait for you early tomorrow morning at the *kastro*, since I have to go to town to help Electra."

So it was just getting light when I went up to Khorio by the shortest route—like stairs between white walls. I hadn't been there a quarter of an hour when we met be-low the *kastro*. She'd told me the truth, she'd had to go to help Electra, who was busy with her baby, but we had time to talk and especially to hug. She was affectionate and sweet but also skittish as a cat, and we followed one another over the cobblestones of the *kastro* amid the first rays of daylight. Her parents were serious people, she told me, and I would have to speak with them. "I certainly will," I said. "There's nothing I want more, if they'll have me." We agreed to talk about it the day after the baptism.

But that night we embraced again because they were holding a strange ceremony that I'd never seen in Trebizond. They burned a doll seated in a chair and wearing a fisherman's hat, which represented Judas. They did it at night, with a lot of ruckus and fireworks. Afterwards, at home, we ate almonds while sipping *ouzo* with cold water. With a candle lit from the Easter candle at church, which his wife had brought home, Yanni traced a cross in smoke on the white ceiling of the entryway.

"It's an old custom," he explained, "and a sign that protects the family."

The next day, we celebrated the baptismal feast in the little olive grove they had between the port and the upper part of town. While everyone was giving little Andreas their blessing, I was pensive. With the smell of the lamb roasting on the spit, whole, and the bitter scent of the herbs, everybody seemed happier and more talkative than me. I was thinking about tomorrow's conversation and planning the best words to convince Yanni. I was very afraid that Alexia's parents wouldn't accept an exile, too young and too poor, for their daughter. I wasn't from Symi, or even Greek.

So that night—they'd made a place for me in Iorgos's room—I decided to confide in my friend. And Iorgos laughed at my fears. He embraced me happily, and on Tuesday you might say that he took care of everything. I hardly had to speak:

"Father, Mother, give Aram a hug. He'll be another son for you."

Then there were, of course, exclamations from her mother, long discussions: we were very young; Alexia didn't have a dowry yet; I didn't care, I wanted her and only her; you have to wait a while. And, at the end, hugs and laughter and *ouzo*.

The next day we were going back to Marseille. In the afternoon, Iorgos and I swore in our own way that we were brothers. Yanni let us take the boat to the bay of Emporios. We dropped anchor and took a few swims around the boat, in the clearest water of any sea in the world.

The only thing that worries me a little is whether Alexia will be able to adapt to the hustle and bustle of Marseille after living in Symi all her life. Will she like Marseille? I guess we'll see when the day comes. If she misses Symi too much, we could always move some-where. A few weeks back, our boat stopped at a town to sell coral—but it didn't seem like a town, more like an island. In fact, the best way to get there is by sea. It's full of well-tended olive trees. The houses aren't as beautiful as those on Symi, it's true, but I think Alexia would feel right at home. The name of this town of fisherman and sailors is Cadaqués.

(Aram's handwriting is no longer found in the journal. He's very young, but also in many respects already a man, and he loses the habit of recording his memories and im-pressions: he leaves the telling—the writing—to Maryk.)

VII
Vahe

Until we lose sight of one another
    May there be peace in the East.
    May armpits drip with sweat,
    not with blood!
    May the smallest village, to the sound of the zither,
    be filled with songs of praise!
    May the land to the West be fertile.
    May every star melt into dew,
    may every seed be cast in gold!
    As the sheep graze on the mountaintops,
    may bud and blossom bloom!
    May abundance shine in the North,
    may the scythe fall endlessly
    into the sea of white wheat!
    And may the barns, opening to the harvest,
    send forth joy!
    In the South may the fruits be without number,
    the honey shine in the heart of the hive,
    may the wine pour out, may the cups run over!
    And when the young wife bakes the good bread,
    may she light up with love!

DANIEL VAROUJAN, "ANDASTAN"

1923
Maryk—Marseille

Today I received a letter from Father Mesrob, of the monastery in Venice where Vahe had studied, and where he had been happy, because living in Venice in an Armenian convent didn't seem to him like exile. I was happy to get it, since Aram has been away for days now, and when I'm alone the memories weigh on me more than ever. I was so moved by the letter from San Lazzaro that I want to copy it in this notebook. It brought back an image of Vahe when he was young, an adolescent, that the years could erase.

Letter of Father Mesrob, of the monastery of San Lazzaro (Venice) to Maryk.

Dear Madam,

After a long time, from first, one of our former students, Dr. Arshag of Yerevan, and then through the Red Cross, I have received news of the death of your dear husband, Vahe, also an ex-student, and of you. I am quite old now, but I never forget my students, much less Vahe: his talent, his sensitivity, his passion for Armenia.

Believe me when I say that, among all the afflictions visited upon our people, the death of poets such as Vahe, Ruben Sevak, and Siamanto is one of the crimes that have pained us the most deeply. All three wanted to create and to fight for the independence of our people. I want to express to you my condolences, as well as those of our entire community, and to assure you that we pray for his immortal soul. As good a man as he was, and a martyred innocent, he certainly rests in the peace of our Lord.

You might say that I witnessed the first blossoming of your husband's poetic vocation, may he rest in peace. At the time, he had a real hunger for knowledge about the history of Armenia, one of the subjects that I taught, and its ancient poetry. I continued to keep up with his life, from a distance, because he was kind enough to send to me his two books and news of his marriage to you and the baptism of his three children. I think he always had fond memories of San Lazzaro, this little piece of Armenia in Italy, his "red earth" in Venice.

Though his first published poems were dedicated to the ancient pagan gods before Armenia's conversion to Christianity, I appreciated them as a testament to the passion for his people, which I have mentioned. It was natural enough in his early youth. As a monk, I don't need to tell you how pleased I was to see his work take a more religious and populist turn. Without the catastrophe that the Turks have inflicted upon Armenia, we would have read new books by Vahe, who was so young when they cut short his life. I have thought many times that he would have been saved if he had chosen to remain in exile, like the poet Chobanian. But perhaps his vocation as a voice of the people might have dried up . . . The ways of human destiny and those of the Lord are inscrutable.

I know you have a son, and I hope that his company, and the knowledge that Vahe's poetry will live forever, will be a source of comfort to you, as will your faith and courage. Dr. Arshag, in his letter to me, spoke very highly of you. If your son should ever wish to spend time with us, to rest, meditate, or recover, we would be delighted to welcome him.

May God and Saint Mekhitar bless you, dear Maryk. Enclosed is a book about our monastery and an old school magazine with a stanza from an early poem by Vahe under the illustration.

> With all the love of Christ, yours,
> Father Mesrob

In the school magazine there is a lovely photograph of the monastery on the island of San Lazzaro, and under it this short verse by Vahe:

> Venice, oh noble dame
> of ocher and of azure,
> Italy intoxicated you with the blood of its vines,
> Oh how they sparkle upon you
> from your forehead to your ankles
> all the jewels of the Orient!
> [Daniel Varoujan, "Venice"]

What a shame that the whole poem isn't there! It's clear that it was from when Vahe was a boy, but I would've liked to read it all. He often told me how he'd missed home while studying at the University of Ghent, where he'd continued his studies, with its gray skies and rain, whereas in Venice he'd hardly missed it at all. It's such a beautiful city; I've never been there. To me, our Trebizond seemed pretty enough, with its blue sea (though they call it black) and the ancient Greek churches, the golden icons, and the smell of incense. Especially, for me, the Armenian Church of Saint Thaddeus, where we were married with crowns of flowers on our heads and fire in our hearts.

I still miss it, my city. And afterwards, like a leaf blown by the wind, like two leaves, Aram and I: Van, Persia, the mountains, Etchmiadzin, Yerevan, and the sea, and Marseille . . . Yerevan, I admit, was a big and handsome city as well, with its pinkish brick houses, but I don't miss it at all because we suffered a lot there, in those dank and smoky rooms. I do remember, though, the fountains, with pure, cool water from the mountains, and the snowy peak of Ararat—our peak, which I will never forget. Also Dr. Arshag's pleasant home, and his favorite saying, "Water from snow, water from God," which he would repeat even though he never turned down a glass of good Armenian cognac when he took time off from the hospital, every once in a while.

These days I'm getting used to the idea of spending the rest of my life in Marseille. Luck would have it that we arrived here knowing we'd have a place to live, even if it's small and on a noisy street. Vahe always dreamed that we would take a trip and that he would take me to the places of his youth: Venice, Paris, Ghent. Who knows? Maybe we would have done it, because he earned a good living, I was frugal, and we even had his parents' place rented out since Grandmother lived with us. We would have gone and come back, instead of this exile without return, without a homeland . . .

Aram never talks to me of those times in Etchmiadzin and Yerevan. He's young, and he only wants to remember the island Symi and his Alexia, Iorgos's sister, to whom he's engaged. I was surprised; it happened so fast, like spring lightning. I'm happy for him, but it makes me feel more alone. Alone and worried when he's at sea, and maybe underwater. My son, the only child I have left.

Father Arshavir has asked me to marry him. I was expecting it. I've told him I can't give him an answer until I speak to Aram when he returns to Marseille. He's resigned to waiting—impatiently, he says—because he loves me very much.

Yesterday I married Arshavir! I would never have done it without my son's consent—if he hadn't approved, or if it hurt him too much.

When I talked to him about it, the day after he returned from Port-Vendres—I let him get a good night's sleep—I had the impression that he wasn't very surprised.

"I could see, Mother, that Father Arshavir was after you, or at least that he liked you a lot, in every way. He always followed you with his eyes. I noticed it a long time ago, the day of the first Armenian party."

"If you don't want me to do it, or if you think I'm disrespectful of your father's memory, I'll tell him that it cannot be," I told him.

But Aram answered that he didn't hold it against me, that I would hold on to the memory of Vahe anyway, that I was still in love with him, and that the decision to marry Arshavir was different:

"I know you're looking for company; you're alone a lot, Mother."

"And I care about him very much; he's a good man."

He smiled and kissed me, and added:

"I could never feel jealous of the Der Baba. I know you're marrying him mostly because of the roses. Maybe you didn't even realize it, but I've seen the way you always look at the roses in the garden, how you touch them . . ."

Aram was exaggerating! He was referring, of course, to the garden of the Armenian church and of the house where we live as of yesterday, which is attached to it. It's actually a rose garden, because there are many kinds: red roses, tea roses, and also little white climbing roses. I love to water the rose bushes, to prune them, to cut a few stems for the icons, to smell the flowers. So Aram has given me his blessing, as they say, because he says a son can't be jealous of roses.

I convinced Aram to live with us while he's on dry land, but he's kept the little apartment on the rue Longue-des-Capucins. He's been fixing it up and repainting it for when he marries his Alexia. Arshavir had taken care of all the paperwork and the necessary steps, so we married early yesterday morning, when the sun had barely risen above the rose bushes and the stained-glass windows.

Now I wear two gold rings. The day I accepted Arshavir's proposal after the Sunday service, he said that he would come and see us for a few moments in the afternoon, before catechism, and that he would bring me a gift. We were amazed, Aram and I, because he came carrying a big package.

"For you, dear Maryk. Aram, you'll like it, too. I don't want it to seem like I'm trying to buy your affection with this surprise."

Arshavir's eyes were ablaze with happiness; he didn't have the serious expression that he usually has. I opened up the package impatiently. The cover of the simple little book stunned me and brought tears to my eyes: *The Unpublished Poems of Vahe: The Song of Armenia*. I could hardly read the titles of the poems I knew by heart: "The Cross of Wheat," "The Threshing Floor," "Until We Lose Sight of One Another." Some time ago Arshavir had asked me to copy them down, this little clutch of golden grain, the book that Vahe hadn't been able to finish himself.

> Golden earth of ripe fruit,
> with my silver sickle
> I shall come
> to reap your gold.

Arshavir and I have many friends in the Armenian community, and even though we didn't want a big party—or think it was fitting—they lavished us with attention and presents. They wouldn't let us prepare anything. It was the women of the parish who cooked a delicious breakfast of cold rice *sarma* wrapped in grape leaves (I don't know where they got so many leaves from!) and seasoned with mint and cinnamon. They also made a heap of pastries with nuts, our *kadaif*, which I hadn't tasted in ages. And they offered bowls of pomegranate seeds preserved in sugar and Armenian wine, all kinds of homemade yogurts, and even more things.

They filled the church with flowers, and the songs rang out.

I didn't want to, but maybe it was inevitable that, once in a while, I thought of my wedding to Vahe. Back then everything was a celebration, we were very young and so in love. I was wearing a white dress, I hardly knew what sorrow was . . . And they sang us the old song of *Anoush*, which once would have been improper for a *der hayr*, or for a widow . . . I've always remembered the beautiful melody:

How much water falls from the clouds,
making puddles on the ground!
Who is the bridegroom of this girl
who cries so bitterly?
—Oh, you cool and crystal breezes
from the mountains blowing down,
crossing plains and deserts,
did my beloved drink of your water?
—Child, your beloved came and went
on fire and bewitched with love.
His ardent heart both came and went,
but left unrefreshed by the cool waters.

Yesterday, since we're in the week of *Vartavar*, the cantors chose a hymn dedicated to Saint Gregory of Narek because they know that I have a special place in my heart for the monastery at Lake Van. I loved it because it speaks of roses, which fits in with our holy day, which means "fire of roses."

My son accompanied me to the altar, and he looked truly handsome, my Aram. But today he left us to go back to work, the work he loves, and that earns him a living. But that still weighs on my heart, though I'm more used to it by now. Now I can talk about this with Arshavir, this good man, and he calms me down.

Aram is out of danger.

He'll be fine, and the doctor has assured me that he won't be an invalid, though there will surely be long-term effects. He says he'll have a slight limp, perhaps for the rest of his life. In fact, he's starting to walk, with some difficulty. He's regained feeling in his left leg, which is the injured one. Today, on my arm, is the first day he went out into the rose garden.

Just when it seemed that our life had calmed down, and he was so happy thinking about his Alexia, everything blew up in our faces. His colleagues—they told me afterwards—said they'd been worried about him for some days. Even the boss, who thinks a lot of him, had advised him to stay on shore because he wasn't his usual self. After the accident they examined the equipment, and it wasn't damaged. So it seems that it was a bad decision on Aram's part: he dove down too far or else came up too fast, which is unlike him. Luckily, Iorgos noticed right away that something was wrong so, as he explained to me, the nitrogen deficiency was no worse.

After the first terribly uncertain days, the doctor saw that Aram would pull through, and he wasn't saying that just to comfort me. My son is brave, and I hope that he'll regain all his strength. He's in good spirits again and beginning to make plans, undaunted by his accident. The thing that most bothers him is that he can't keep diving, because this job requires excellent physical condition. So Mr. Kontos's visit yesterday was providential.

"Don't worry about the job, Aram," he assured him. "Diving isn't everything."

"What do you mean?"

"That you have a lot of experience at sea, you're a quick learner. There'll always be work for you in our company no matter what. You can be an excellent guide on deck because you know the other side of the sea."

"I think I'd like that a lot."

"So work on getting better, and you can count on it. Adonis is getting older and says he wants to retire and go back to Symi. You know he has a house there and his own fishing tackle."

I think this prospect was the best medicine for Aram! Arshavir had suggested that since Aram knew a lot about books and accounts, though he hadn't spent much time in school, he might find him a job with the church's mutual aid society. But I couldn't imagine my son in an office job, even with his disability, and I hadn't mentioned it to him. He who was only happy at sea!

I know what caused his accident: it's the past that's forever weighing us down. I regret not having persuaded him to stay home for a few days. I did try, but he wouldn't listen. Maybe I should've insisted, but my son is a grown man, despite his youth. Aram wasn't as alert as he should have been because he couldn't get the death of his father, our Vahe, out of his head. It was one thing to know about it in a vague way, and another the shock of the cold, hard facts. Besides, he'd shielded himself with his own imagination, picturing Vahe as one of the rebels who had joined Ruben's army. How could he have joined their ranks? By force of will Aram had convinced himself that his father had died in combat against the Turkish executioners, weapons in hand. But Vahe had no weapon other than his poetry.

Now the reports have been made public, to the shame and disgrace of our executioners. When Yanek, the widow of the poet Ruben Sevak, came to see us along with Odysseus, my husband's Greek colleague, a professor at the same school, we still didn't know how they'd killed him and his friends—how they'd murdered them. Joseph Burtt, who's collecting information for his book on "the people of Ararat," paid for Odysseus's trip from Athens to Paris. He says that a publisher in London, Hogarth Press, will publish the book. Because now Odysseus is an exile, too, since the Turks expelled all the Greeks from "New Turkey" and killed the Greeks of Smyrna. Fortunately, Odysseus managed to save himself and now teaches in Greece, but the Turks took everything from him.

It's the only time in our whole life that I've seen the beloved face of my son, with his velvet eyes, turn into a mask of rage. It lasted for only a few minutes, as he was reading the testimony of Hassan—the Turkish taxi driver who was an involuntary witness to Vahe's death. Then tears washed away the hate, but happiness has still not returned to his eyes. I hope that Alexia will be able to bring it back.

We'd been told that Yanek and Odysseus would be visiting Marseille, and I'd prepared a good dinner at home. They said they didn't want me to bother, that we could go to a restaurant for bouillabaisse, but I refused. We may be far from our homeland, but we shouldn't lose the Armenian tradition of hospitality. Odysseus said that he wanted to speak with Arshavir first, and they went into his study. Afterwards, out of discretion, Arshavir said he was going to eat with a friend of his, the lead singer of the church choir, so he wasn't at the meal. Aside from Aram—young people are always hungry—those of us around the table had no appetite, though they praised the stuffed grape leaves, our *dolma*, which had come out so well. While we ate we talked about our adventures, our flight from Van, and Yanek's long train journey through wartime Europe with her months-old son, because she'd left when things began. After dinner I served strong coffee and candied nuts. Up until that moment we'd avoided, by tacit agreement, saying Vahe's name. Arshavir came back in time to drink a cup of coffee and went off to his office, saying that he had work to catch up on.

The professor, whom I remembered from our good times in Trebizond, showed an interest in my son's work. He swore that he would never have recognized him if it hadn't been for his eyes. I finished pouring the coffee and sat down, because it was time to face the truth about the death of our Vahe. Odysseus linked it to what he'd said about my boy:

"So, yes, I would've recognized your eyes. You have the same eyes as your father, my friend."

And he went on:

"Maryk, Aram, I have to tell you about Vahe's last days. I know you're brave, Maryk. I was one of the last to see him, because they arrested us on the same day. He was in prison for a long time."

Yanek took my hand and said:

"I'm in the same situation as you: they killed my Ruben in the same way."

Then, Odysseus added, to console us before we heard terrible words:

"I can assure you that, while he was in prison, they never tortured him, as they did others. He even asked me to have his *Iliad* brought to him to read, and I did. A sign that he was well. Luckily, his last day was short. Much shorter than the interminable days of those who were sent to die in the desert."

Odysseus gulped down his coffee and told me, in a few words, that Vahe, along with five other prisoners, was knifed to death on the pretext of a transfer to another prison. Then Odysseus handed me a few folded sheets of paper, because the truth is that his voice was breaking. He couldn't go on. Aram stood and put his arm around my back and stroked my hair. I put on my glasses, and my son waited for me to finish reading and hand him the papers. I had to dry my glasses over and over.

Just when Aram had finished reading, Arshavir came in and took us both in his arms as we cried and cried. He had the sense to say nothing, but it was obvious that Odysseus had explained things to him before when they'd been alone in his office. Afterwards, he poured us both a glass of cognac, which he was hardly in the habit of doing. After a while, when they saw that we were calmer, Odysseus and Yanek took their leave. They had another visit to make in Marseille. Arshavir timidly asked if I wanted to go to church with him for a bit, and I did. Aram stayed by himself. When I found him, it was getting dark, and he hadn't even turned on the lights.

The next day, despite my pleas, he returned to the boat.

"Mother, what do you want me to do? Work is the only thing that can help me. If I stay here, it'll be worse. I could join the Armenian Revolutionary Federation to avenge Father's death, who knows! You wouldn't want me turning into a Dashnak."

"Aram," I cried, " your father isn't dead."

"I know, Mother, that his poetry will live forever, while no one remembers the filthy names of the bastards who killed him. But they did kill him."

And with a hug he ran off, so I wouldn't see the tears in his eyes.

Now I'll sew into the diary, which is running out of pages, the reports from Odysseus and Hassan, so that the memory remains forever. The memory of Vahe, the memory of his death: thus died a son of Armenia.

Testimony of Odysseus X to the American Commission

I was a professor of mathematics at X high school, and a colleague and close friend of Vahe's.

They arrested me, by mistake, the same day as the three Armenian professors and the Armenian doctors of this nationality. It was the beginning of the persecution. I was able to show that I was Greek, though my mother was Armenian. They let me go the same day, without making me bring in my father. They left my mother alone, because they consider that a married woman adopts her husband's nationality.

The official who let me go was rather deferential, and I took advantage of this to assist, to the limited extent that I could, my friend Vahe. He proved responsive to my offers; in so many words, I bribed him to make sure they didn't torture my colleagues, and I promised him more if he managed to get word from my friend, the poet. We still had no idea of the crime being planned against Armenia.

"Agreed," he said in a low voice, amid the confusion in that section of the prison. "But don't come here, it's too dangerous. I'll go to your house myself."

I also offered to teach mathematics to his son, for free, if he was having problems in school.

The inspector kept his word. I recognized Vahe's handwriting, shakier, in pencil, on a scrap of wrapping paper:

"I'm fine. Reassure my mother. There are lots of us and we suffer from the heat. Could you get me a little fresh fruit and my *Iliad*."

I quieted his mother's fears as best I knew how. His wife and son were away, at the monastery of Narek near Van. More than once in the following weeks, I sent clean clothes and fruit to my colleagues from school, but I received only one more laconic message from Vahe:

"Thank you, brother."

That was so typical of him, it was so affectionate, that it shook me. I had no illusions about how the incarceration of the Armenians would end; I remembered the earlier massacres. They would kill them. You don't have to be a mathematician to calculate the probabilities of a bad or a good outcome. The news was more disturbing every day.

The inspector was, in his way, rather honorable. He accepted money, but in return for certain efforts. So I was worried when he came to my house one evening and returned the money I'd given him that week:

"Take this, it isn't mine; I have no right to it."

"Why?" My voice would barely come out.

"I can do no more for your friend," he said. "They've punished me for my 'leniency' and are sending me to a smaller village where there are no Armenians. Those are the orders from above. Tomorrow your friends will be transferred. I don't want to be involved in what's being planned." He stopped for a second.

"I was able to find out what the orders are. Your friend will die on the way; they'll kill them all. I'm sorry, he was a good person."

I hadn't heard incorrectly. He'd said "was." In the eyes of the police, my friend was already sentenced, dead. So we could do nothing to save him. There was only one thing that I could still do in his memory: to carry his death, the secret of his death, with me. To say not one word to his mother. So I didn't worry her; the waters of the Black Sea, a short time later, forever hid from her the death of her child, my friend Vahe.

Testimony of Hassan, Turkish Taxi Driver

I committed homicide. I killed a man and paid my debt to justice with fifteen years' hard labor. I was very young. But I killed him face-to-face, in a brawl. I'm neither a coward nor a murderer, like the ones I've seen in action.

The police told me that at a certain hour of the morning, very early, I had to be available in the usual place. My taxi is big. They threatened that if I didn't do it, with my record, there would be serious consequences. When I got there, there was already another big car carrying a policeman and five *effendis*. Two gendarmes arrived on foot. One of the *effendis* was a young man, with a black beard and bright eyes. They were all well dressed but seemed defeated, their hands tightly bound.

The policeman in charge made them get into my car, and he and the gendarmes followed us in the other taxi. We took the inland road. All of a sudden, in a clearing, we came to a halt. A group of five armed men blocked our way. They tied my hands and the hands of the other taxi driver and made the five *effendis* get out of the car, yelling at them to give up everything they were carrying. But how could they, if their hands were bound? The police searched them and took everything they had, which wasn't much—a few bills, coins, a tobacco pouch, the rosaries.

It's for sure that the policeman made an agreement with the leader of the bandits; he whispered in his ear. I think they decided to split what little booty there was. The victims must have seen what was coming. The police took some stuff, untied the other taxi driver, and left. To me, the whole thing was a setup, it was all planned in advance. Why else would they have been such cowards?

The bandits untied my hands and told me to go back to the city if I knew what was good for me, while they took the five prisoners away. I disobeyed them because I could see their bad intentions: I drove slowly, following them from a distance, and watched what was happening. But they left the highway, crossed a dried-up stream, and went as far as the little hill by the road. This hill is covered with trees, but they didn't even go into the woods. As soon as they got to the first trees, the leader of the band shouted some things I didn't understand, because I wasn't close enough. When they heard that, the bandits fell on the *effendis*, and it all went very fast.

I stopped the car—they had other things to do than look at me. They fell on the *effendis*, tore at their clothes, and undressed them, leaving them as naked as the day they were born. The poor victims, defenseless, their hands tied once more, were beaten and hung, one per tree. Then they pulled out their knives, and, to the horrible screams of those innocents, they stabbed them in cold blood, over and over. Their helpless screams broke my heart. That's how they died, all five of them, stabbed, unable to defend themselves.

Aram never wrote in his diary again. In any case, as Maryk observed, there wasn't any space left. If he ever bought a new one, we'll never know. I find only a few lines in Maryk's hand. Even if I can't understand them, Maria Ohannesian, the translator, has taught me to distinguish the two handwritings. The mother writes simply, on an empty line on the last page:

"Today we returned from Symi, from Aram's wedding."

I'm not sure who she's referring to with this plural, *we*. To herself, Aram, Arshavir, and Alexia? To herself, the *der hayr*, and other Armenian friends? That could be, because Greek weddings are quite open and often huge. And we've already seen that the Kontos family was generous and welcoming. Perhaps Aram stayed longer on the island because the relatives wanted to fete the newlyweds and make the party last. I imagine a joyous wedding, in a church near the port, or maybe even in the monastery of Saint Michael Panormitis, with the bells in the beautiful bell tower ringing out in Symi's crystalline air.

If Aram and Alexia in fact spent more time on the island with the Kontos family, Maryk and her husband could easily have returned to Marseille on one of the boats that regularly sailed from the neighboring island of Rhodes. I think it was about time for Maryk to take a trip without anguish or fear.

I couldn't feel satisfied, though, without knowing more about my coral fisherman. How is it, I wondered, that the Kontos family kept Aram's diary? Maybe Aram and Alexia had no children. Iorgos was clearly like a brother to Aram, but if Alexia had been a mother, I thought, the diary would have ended up in the hands of her children. I even imagined a possible result of his accident, that he suffered consequences more painful than his limp. Another thing I don't know is whether Aram and Alexia always lived in Marseille. The boy seemed doubtful that his island girl could adapt to the big city. I don't know, then, if they settled in Cadaqués or, when they were older, went back to sunny little Symi after the island was liberated from the Italians and the Turks— when it officially became what it had always been: a Greek rock through and through. Because Iorgos himself settled down in Cadaqués and so must have given the boats, nets, and his father's trade to Aram and Alexia, his brother and sister.

One thing seems highly likely: Aram went back to diving, if only once. Because in the year 1924 Commandant de Corlieu invented the swim fins that are so familiar to us now. That's when the frogman was born, and our friend's limp, under water, ceased to exist. But this is all conjecture. If I have to go by the diary, I know only that I left Aram with the death of his father engraved on his heart. Vahe's death, which was sung by the waters of the sea before they knew that his son would one day fish there for coral, the beautiful *Corallium rubrun*:

> Having vanquished you, Poseidon,
> the sea is a great void.
> you will never again cross her forests of coral,
> and the rebel dolphin
> no longer fears your trident.

Epilogue

There is another, more disturbing, possibility: that Aram gave his diary to his friend because he chose a dangerous path. It could very well be that he joined one of the armed resistance groups in the Armenian diaspora, resolved to fight for the independence of his people and to bring the murderers to justice—the murderers of Vahe.

Because after the first trials, Turkish leaders backtracked and tried to turn history around. Not only did they deny any reparations or justice to the Armenian people; there was no genocide at all, they said at first. Or, if there were any massacres, they were sporadic, or directed at small groups of rebels. In other words, there were none, and, in the end, it turns out that there had never been any Armenians in Armenia!

So a number of children and grandchildren of the thousands of victims took to direct action and to attempts on the lives of Turkish diplomats, the "guardians of negation," those who protest wherever—in Marseille, in the United States—Armenians build a monument to remember their dead. Those who black out the name of Armenia on a Swiss map, those who carry out the order to erase history. I cannot confirm whether or not

Aram became a Dashnak, but that possibility cannot be excluded. I recall his admiration for the rebels of Musa Dagh and what he told his mother: that if he didn't go to sea, he'd become a revolutionary. It seems probable, then, that Aram stayed on in Marseille and that, if not he himself, then his descendants might have aligned themselves with this militant orientation. Alexia, a daughter of Greece, a people who loved liberty, would not have been opposed to such a position. Not all of this springs from my imagination, as you will soon see.

While I was preparing this book, I consulted many French newspapers, as well as publications of the Armenian diaspora, in which there were many articles in French written by the new generations born in France. I also got hold of publications from the time of the Second World War to look for Armenian surnames. I remembered quite well that in the years of the genocide, during the First World War, from 1914 to 1918, Turkey was an ally of the Germans.

Among the articles from those years, I found one that was striking. Missak Manouchian, an orphan who had escaped the massacres of 1915, was at the time a well-known journalist. He joined the French Resistance and distinguished himself at the head of a commando unit made up of foreigners for the audacity of his sabotage campaigns around Paris. He and his whole group fell into the hands of the Nazis and were killed by firing squad in February 1944.

The daring of this group, and of others, revealed to my mind a certain experience of clandestine action, surely in the bosom of the Armenian Revolutionary Federation. Times had changed, and the names of the combatants were not just names of men. Thousands of Armenians, including girls and women, entered the ranks of the Resistance. And among these names I see another that touches me: Louise Aslanian, the same last name as Aram.

Louise hadn't joined the group alone. I was arrested first by her name, because it's a girl's name, but I look at each name more closely and I read: Arpiar and Louise Aslanian, brother and sister.* Were they, Louise and Arpiar, heroic fighters against the Nazis, perhaps the children of Aram and Alexia, and therefore the grandchildren of Maryk and Vahe?

---

*Translator's note: Though the author believes that Arpiar and Louise Aslanian were brother and sister, they were in fact a married couple, as well as prominent anti-fascists and members of the French Resistance. Arpiar met his end in February 1945, after being deported to the Nazi concentration camp Dora-Mittelbau; Louise died at the Nazi Ravensbrück camp nearly two weeks earlier.

Author's Note

The book is a work of fiction, but the events of the genocide were, unfortunately, all too real. Also real is the testimony of Hassan regarding the deaths of Ruben Sevak and Daniel Varoujan. His words were recorded by an Armenian priest and can be found in the book *Persecutions against Armenian Doctors*, published in Constantinople in 1919. Daniel Varoujan did ask for *The Iliad* while in prison. The word "genocide," which you will not find in Aram's diary, was first used at Nuremberg to define in one word the crimes of the Nazis against humanity.

I have allowed myself some leeway with time. For example, I place Aram and Maryk in Marseille in 1921, whereas the majority of the Armenian refugees in Greece stayed in that hospitable country from 1922 until 1924.

The Greek coral divers in my account are loosely based on the figure of Iorgos Kontos and his family, the coral fishermen from Symi whom the Catalan author Josep Pla depicts in his 1966 collection *Aigua de mar* and whose children and grandchildren live in Cadaqués. The first Kontos arrived in Barcelona in 1900 to train the divers of the Spanish fleet.

There is extensive information about the Armenian Genocide in the books by Dr. Yves Ternon, *La cause arménienne* (1983) and *L'état criminel: Les génocides au XXe siècle* (1995), as well as Christopher Walker's *Armenia: The Survival of a Nation* (1980). As for the Kurds, although some tribes had assisted the Turks in the genocide, they soon understand that their case is similar to that of the Armenians and sign a pact in Paris, but to no avail. With the intensification of Turkish imperialism, the Kurdish people will suffer almost the same fate as Armenia. The Turkish government represses Kurdish uprisings with blood and fire; it also plans a program of genocide comparable to that which has occupied us in this story, this time based on the "technique" of deportation to the high mountains in the middle of winter. This program is applied to half a million Kurds. In the end, a million and a half Kurds have been victims of it. Today, in 1997, the genocide of the Kurdish people continues.

On the other hand, Nazim Bey was executed in 1926—the only one of the leaders of the genocide who did not die by Armenian hands. Nazim had become involved in a plot against the new ruler of Turkey, the modernizer Mustafa Kemal Ataturk. He was tried and condemned to death in Smyrna in 1925. At Nazim's first trial in Constantinople in the year 1919, Ataturk, then a young soldier, had been summoned as a witness and did not mince words: "Our compatriots have committed unheard-of crimes, through every imaginable form of despotism; they have organized mass deportations, they have burned babies alive in their cribs, raped women . . ." Nazim's death in 1926 must have seemed to him doubly just, deferred as it was for seven years.

The author would like to thank Maria Ohanessian, Armenian and Hellenist, for her invaluable advice.

A Select Historical Chronology

I. Some Historical Antecedents

Ninth century BCE: Settlement of Urartu, on the Anatolian plateau, by the people who would later become ethnic Armenians. Various Assyrian invasions.

Fourth century BCE: Armenia conquered by Alexander the Great; later becomes a Roman province.

First century CE: The apostles Jude Thaddeus and Bartholomew introduce Christianity to Armenia; the Armenian Church thus comes to be called "Apostolic" and, alternatively, Gregorian.

Fourth century CE: The Armenian nation adopts Christianity under the influence of Saint Gregory the Illuminator. Saint Mesrop Mashtots creates the Armenian alphabet.

Fifth century CE: Armenia is divided between Persia and Byzantium.

Tenth century CE: First Armenian cultural renaissance. Emergence of the great poet Gregory of Narek, the son of the bishop and theologian Khosrov the Great. Armenia is annexed by the Byzantine Empire, and Turkish and Mongolian invasions begin.

1263–1375: In the region of Cilicia, Armenians from the valley of the Euphrates found the Kingdom of Little Armenia, with which the Kingdom of Catalonia establishes close commercial, diplomatic, and familial relations. Ramon Llull visits Cilicia; in 1331 the last Armenian king of Cilicia, Leo IV, marries the Catalan princess Constance of Sicily.

1473: Western Armenia is absorbed by the Ottoman Empire.

Fifteenth century CE: The Armenian Catholicos returns to the See of Etchmiadzin in eastern Armenia.

Fifteenth and sixteenth centuries CE: Great flourishing of Armenian troubadours and other poets. The major poet Nahapet Kuchak lives from 1500 to 1592.

1639: The Ottoman Turks and Persians divide Armenia between them, signing a pact to this effect.

1742: Armenian Patriarchate is created in Lebanon.

1878: Eastern Armenia is incorporated into czarist Russia. A short time after, the Turks introduce 100,000 Kurds into Armenian territory, who proceed to wreak havoc on the Armenian population. Armenian resistance to Ottoman rule slowly increases.

Twentieth century CE: War and genocide [see below]. Centered in Istanbul, Armenian modernist literature flowers in the century's first decades. The so-called Mehian group forms, which includes Vahan Tekeyan, Hrand Nazariantz, Daniel Varoujan, Ruben Sevak, Arshag Chobanian, and Siamanto (Adom Yarjanian). Sevak, Siamanto, and Varoujan are imprisoned at the start of the genocide and murdered in 1915.

December 2, 1920: The Treaty of Alexandropol forces Armenia to cede all former Ottoman territories granted under the Treaty of Sèvres.

1922: Armenia is annexed by and incorporated into the Union of Soviet Socialist Republics.

1936–38: Stalinist purges and terror. Armenian Catholicos Khoren I is assassinated by the Soviet NKVD.

1991: Amid the fall of communism and geopolitical upheavals, Armenia declares its statehood as an independent republic.

The traditional Armenian homeland on the Anatolian plateau continues to be erased from the map.

II. The Genocide

1876: The "internationalization" of the Armenian question begins. The Armenian Church maintains and consolidates the national spirit in lieu of territorial boundaries. The soldier Abdul Hamid persecutes and deports Armenians, repopulating six Armenian provinces with Circassian immigrants.

1887: The Armenians create the nationalist party Hunchak.

1894: Creation of the Armenian Revolutionary Federation.

1894–96: Abdul Hamid orders the massacre of Armenians; 200,000 Armenians die as foreign powers are slow to react.

1908: The Young Turk Revolution.

1909: New massacres in Adana (Cilicia); 30,000 Armenians die.

April 1915 (World War I, 1914–18): Within two days, 2,345 notable Constantinopolitan Armenians (doctors, professors, political leaders) are imprisoned under the pretext that a corps of Armenian volunteers is serving the Russian army. The majority of these individuals are murdered.

1915–16: Genocide against the Armenians is organized by the Turkish government, which, under the political regime of the doctors Nazim and Shakir and supervised by the Ministry of the Interior under Talaat Pasha, has trained common criminals and *četés* (armed mercenary brigands).

Armenians are annihilated in various ways (firing squad, burning alive, starvation, forced marches in the desert, drownings in the Black Sea, etc.). An estimated 1.6 million Armenians die. Many girls and boys are raped or stolen from their families.

October 15, 1915: The viscount James Bryce presents a report to the Chamber of Lords in England regarding the genocide against the Armenians, which included numerous eyewitness accounts.

1920: The Treaty of Sèvres (July 10, 1920) recognizes Armenia's right to independence and delimits its new borders. Any Armenian state should include the historic settlements of Erzerum, Trebizond, Van, and Bitlis, including a slice of the Black Sea shore. But such a plan proves untenable. Bryce presents a revised and enlarged report with new testimony: *Armenian Attrocities: The Extermination of a Nation.*

1929: The Near Eastern Relief Society ceases its activities, having agreed with the Soviet government in 1922 to assist refugees in the Caucasus, particularly the education of orphans. American assistance in the NER totaled 28 million dollars. Over 120,000 children are orphaned in the Armenian Genocide.

Glossary of Terms, Names, and Places

Armenian, Turkish, and Greek Terms

Anoush: A five-act opera composed by Armen Tigranian, based on the 1892 poem of the same name by Hovhannes Tumanyan

Catholicos: The chief bishop and spiritual head of Armenian Apostolic Church

Dashnak: A member of the Armenian Revolutionary Federation, also known as the Dashnaktsutyun

der hayr: Armenian priest

effendi: A title of respect in Turkey and former lands of the Ottoman Empire

hadig: An *agra hadig* or *atam hatik*; an Armenian ceremony to commemorate a newborn baby's first tooth

kadaif: Very thin, sweet Turkish noodles used in the dessert of the same name, similar to baklava

kastro: Castle (Greek)

khorovadz: Traditional Armenian barbecue, usually reserved for festive occasions or celebrations

mante: Small, boat-shaped Armenian dumplings served with broth, yogurt, and sumac

ouzo: Anise-flavored Greek drink, similar to raki or arak

sarma: Grape leaves stuffed with aromatic rice

Vartavar: Armenian celebration held fourteen weeks after Easter to commemorate the Transfiguration of Christ

Historical Figures

Burtt, Joseph (1818–1876): Author of a 1925 report on Armenian refugees in the Near East who went on to publish *The People of Ararat*, which was privately printed by Leonard and Virginia Woolf in London the following year. Burtt described the book's intention as "the peremptory need to reawaken the reluctant national consciousness once more to our responsibility on the matter, before it is too late to rescue the perishing remnant in Syria and Greece."

Enver Pasha (1881–1922): Ottoman military officer, revolutionary, and convicted war criminal.

Gregory the Illuminator (240–332 CE): Patron saint and first official head of the Armenian Apostolic Church, responsible for converting Armenia from paganism to Christianity.

Kuchak, Nahapet (?–1592 CE): Armenian poet who was considered one of the first Armenian troubadours. Likely born in village of Kharakonis, near the city of Van.

Mashtots, Mesrop (362–440 CE): Early medieval Armenian theologian, composer, and inventor of the Armenian alphabet.

Talaat Pasha (1874–1921): Ottoman politician and convicted war criminal who planned and executed the Armenian Genocide while serving as the Ottoman Empire's minister of interior affairs; later became grand vizier.

Tehlirian, Soghomon (1896–1960): Armenian revolutionary and soldier who assassinated Talaat Pasha, the former grand vizier of the Ottoman Empire, in Berlin in 1921.

Place Names

Adana: Major city in southern Turkey at the center of
the former Armenian Kingdom of Cilicia (1199–1375)
and site of the 1909 Adana Massacre of Armenians by
Ottoman Muslims. The city and its vilayet would later
form a locus of mass deportations during the Armenian
Genocide.

Ararat (Mount): Highest mountain in modern-day Turkey
and the symbolic heart of historic Armenia, though it
now lies outside its present-day borders.

Cadaqués: Port city on the Cap de Creus peninsula of the
Upper Empordà region of Catalonia

Etchmiadzin: Center of Armenian Apostolic Church,
established 301 CE, and the location of the Armenian
Cathedral and Holy See (Catholicos).

Musa Dagh: Mountain in the Hatay province of Turkey and
the site of armed resistance by local Armenian commu-
nities during the genocide in 1915, which served as the
inspiration for Franz Werfel's novel *The Forty Days of
Musa Dagh*.

San Lazzaro: Island in the Venetian lagoon and, since 1717,
the site of an Armenian Mekhitarist order monastery,
which is one of the world's preeminent centers of
study of Armenian culture.

Tiflis (Tbilisi): Capital of Georgia and a major seat of nine-
teenth-century Armenian culture.

Trebizond (Trabzon): City on the coast of the Black Sea in
northern Turkey where Greek and Armenian commu-
nities that date to the Byzantine period persisted amid

Ottoman rule. A site of Hamidian massacres in 1895, the city's Armenian citizens were subject to arrest, murder, and deportation with the start of the genocide in 1915. During the Turkish War of Independence, the Pontic Greek community suffered mass expulsion and forced population exchange.

Van: City in modern-day eastern Turkey on the shores of Lake Van and the historical center of the Armenian Kingdom of Vaspurakan and site of numerous Armenian monasteries.

Yerevan: Capital and largest city of modern Armenia and one of the world's oldest continually inhabited cities.

Poetry Sources

Nazariantz, Hrand. "The Shepherds of Van." Translated into Catalan by Alfons Maseras. Revista del Centre de Lectura, 1921.

Varoujan, Daniel. "Andastan" [Անդաստան] (1914). https://armenian-poetry.blogspot.com/2015/05/live-from-holy-cross-george-wallace.html.

Varoujan, Daniel. "Benediction." From Հացին Երգը. Published posthumously in Constantinople, 1921.

Varoujan, Daniel. "Red Soil" [Կարմիր Հողը]. From Ցեղին Սիրտը. Constantinople, 1909.

Varoujan, Daniel. "Venice" [Վենետիկ]. From Հեթանոս Երգեր. Constantinople, 1912.

About the Author

Maria Àngels Anglada (1920–1999) was a Catalan poet and author. Following a degree in Classical Philology from the Universitat de Barcelona, she went on to great success as a poet and novelist in her native tongue. Her first novel, *Les closes* (1979), won the prestigious Josep Pla Award, and her novel *Sandàlies d'escuma* (Sandals of Foam), garnered the Lletra d'Or. Her award-winning novel *The Violin of Auschwitz* (1994) has been translated into fourteen languages, while its follow-up based on the Armenian Genocide, *Aram's Notebook* (*El quadern d'Aram*), has been translated into Armenian, French, Italian, and Dutch. Her Catalan translations of the Armenian poet Daniel Varoujan were published posthumously in 2001. Several streets, squares, parks, and avenues across Catalonia—from Vic to Figueres to Girona—have been renamed in honor of Àngels Anglada, and the Government of Catalonia awarded her the Creu de Sant Jordi in 1994. The University of Girona has maintained a Chair of Literary Patrimony in her name since 2004.

S W A N
I S L E
P R E S S

Swan Isle Press is a not-for-profit publisher of literature
in translation including fiction, nonfiction, and poetry.

For information on books of related interest
or for a catalog of Swan Isle Press titles:
www.swanislepress.com

Aram's Notebook
Book and cover design by Marianne Jankowski
Typeset in Libre Caslon Text and
Adobe Jensen Pro Display.